Adventuring
through the
Mirror

For now we see in a mirror dimly, but then face to face;
now I know in part, but then I shall know fully just as I
also have been fully known." I Corinthians 13:12
(New American Standard Bible)

ROSEMARY ANDREWS 7-20

ISBN 978-1-64191-020-0 (paperback)
ISBN 978-1-64191-021-7 (digital)

Christian Faith Publishing, Inc.
832 Park Avenue
Meadville, PA 16335
www.christianfaithpublishing.com

Printed in the United States of America

Contents

Saturday Morning

It was Saturday morning. Something jarred him from a deep sleep. It was so immediate that he sat straight up in bed. His heart was pounding as he looked around the 5:00 a.m. dimness to see if someone had entered the bedroom. The room was still and no bogeyman materialized as his eyes grew accustomed to the shapes and shadows outlined from the night-light near the bathroom door. He fell back onto his pillow, annoyed now that his one day to sleep in was snatched away. He sighed, pulled the coverlet over his face, and tried to force more sleep. Once the tossing and turning started and his wife began sighing in her sleep beside him, he knew it was time to start his day. It was, after all, her only day to sleep in too. They tried, mostly in vain, to train the kids to get their own cereal on Saturdays and toddle off to the game room to watch cartoons until one or the other of them woke up. Usually, a minor skirmish that only Mom or Dad could fix would break out long before either of them had time to rouse from sleep naturally. But this morning, it was way too early for any of that.

Ron slipped on his robe and glanced back at his wife. She was beautiful even in sleep. He thought he could see a half smile on her face as if she subconsciously knew he was up and had everything under control so she could sleep peacefully those precious extra hours.

Before going downstairs, he slipped into the boys' room. How could they look so innocent in those ten and eight-year-old bodies? He knew better. But there they were, completely at peace and still naïve to the peril and naysayers of doom throughout the world. He wanted to ruffle their hair but was afraid that would wake them. Now that he was up, he was starting to covet this private, uninterrupted time to himself. He walked into the girls' room and, as always, did a double take as he looked down at them. They both looked just like their mother with their ivory complexions and delicate features. Their two-year-old still slept in a crib. He liked that. Those surrounding bars gave him a sense of added security around her. He walked over and looked down at their six-year old and could not resist pushing a long, dark wave of hair out of her face. "Thank you, Father-God," he whispered.

He went downstairs and began the usual morning routine: hitting brew on the coffee maker, flipping the switch on the gas fireplace, and adding a few more nuggets into the cat dish, hoping that would stop the meowing. He opened the front door, glancing about to see if the paperboy might have already delivered. No such luck. With a steaming cup of coffee in hand, he headed to the desk in his den and turned on that fireplace as he walked by. Desk equals work, and that was not a priority this morning so he quickly changed his mind and eased down into his well-worn, leather chair instead. This gave him a prime view through the French doors out to the private patio. Trouble was, it was too dark to see. Begrudgingly, he unwound his crossed feet from the ottoman and rose to flip on the porch light. Then he eased back into his chair and relaxed into the stillness for some contemplative time.

He had been wondering for a while and was becoming increasingly perplexed with how little he really knew. Every time he wrangled with yet another biblical concept, it seemed to open up the door to a hundred more questions, and he was no theologian. He was just an ordinary, all-American kind of guy with a high-paying job as an attorney, great wife, and four kids in a beautiful home in a beautiful neighborhood living the American dream. Although he chose not to consciously think of the economic turmoil affecting the entire nation, he was nonetheless cognizant of it and gave thanks daily where thanks was due—to his heavenly Father. God had chosen to continuously bless them with their daily bread and, more often than not, marmalade on top. But something was missing. He wanted more. He needed more. Not materially, but within himself. He had heard that everyone has a hole in his heart that only God can fill. He filled that hole many years ago. He was blessed that both he and his wife were Christians, involved in a Spirit-filled church, and training up their children in the way they should go. But there was still an elusive something that evaded his understanding. "Holy Spirit, please come more fully into my life," he prayed.

He reached over for his Bible just as the doorbell rang. Out of habit, he glanced down at his watch, rolling his eyes when he realized it wasn't on his wrist. No more than twenty minutes could have gone by since he poured his coffee. Who in the world would be ringing their bell this early in the morning? He waited and listened. Maybe he was hearing things. No, it chimed again. Taking no chances, he walked over to his gun cabinet and opened the bottom drawer with the key he kept hidden in a wooden puzzle box. Only he knew the correct twists and turns to the puzzle so only he could open it and retrieve the key. He walked cautiously down the hallway and into the darkened entryway, pistol in hand. He could see a figure through the cut glass window of the front door and flipped on the porch light, giving him the advantage.

"Yes?" he called out. No response. "Can I help you?" he ventured. Still no response. The bell chimed again.

He was going to have to open the door just to silence the chiming before the whole house was roused. He positioned the gun so it hung down by his side but still pointed straight ahead, figuring he could at least maim the intruder if he made a move. He opened the door a few inches and peered out. Standing before him was a fine-looking gentleman in an expensive gray suit with an open-collared, crisply starched shirt in a muted hue of purple. Ron relaxed a little, figuring the man was lost and seeing the light on in the den, stopped to ask directions. He was an imposing man with startling blue eyes and a shag of white hair that was somehow casual yet coiffured. His face reflected complete composure, like someone who had figured out the meaning of life the day he was born, therefore nothing ever rattled him. Ron realized he was looking up at the man, which was saying something since Ron was six two.

It started to become awkward the longer they looked at each other without speaking. Ron blushed a little when he realized he was staring. But the circumstances of someone ringing his bell at this early hour and then finding this extraordinary man standing on his front stoop had caused him to forget his manners. "May I help you?"

The man grinned. It was a warm, magnetic smile that seemed to light up the whole porch with triple the wattage of the shining electric bulbs.

"I believe it is just the opposite. May I help you?"

"Help me?"

"You are Ron Miller."

That was somewhat disconcerting to Ron because the man had not asked a question but had made a firm statement. "Yes. Yes, I am."

"I believe you asked for my assistance a few moments ago."

"Assistance?" Ron was dumbstruck. What was this all about?

"I believe your exact words were 'come more fully into your life'."

Ron's mind was spinning. *A few moments ago? Come more fully into my life? Assistance?* This wasn't making any sense at all. Maybe this guy was a wacko after all. No way was he going to invite him into his home, lost or not. Wait, he was beginning to recall the words. What did he say? It was something about asking the Holy Spirit to come more fully into his life. The realization of what this man might be implying caused his muscles to go lax and the gun dropped with a thud on the floor.

The gentleman grinned again as he stooped to pick it up. "I don't think you will be needing this." He reached out to hand it back to Ron, but Ron had somehow lost control of his leg muscles and slipped down to the floor himself. The visitor leaned in and literally scooped him up in his strong arms and placed him gently on the sofa. He placed the gun on the end table and closed the front door. Then he sat down in the easy chair beside Ron, placing a small, green satchel at his feet.

Ron had not noticed the satchel until now. He looked from it to the visitor and back again, becoming apprehensive about its contents. Still unable to speak, all he could do was stare. The gentleman seemed to have a perpetual grin on his face. His eyes danced with light as if he were inwardly laughing at a joke that only he was in on. He sat patiently, staring back at Ron and waiting for him to gather his wits about him.

Ron stared at him in amazement. "Are you implying that you are the, uh, the Holy…" Ron could not continue. It was too crazy and too far-fetched to even imagine.

"I am not implying anything. I Am."

Ron felt himself blanch. He knew he could not run from this nut job, his muscles were still not cooperating. He was expert in the art of communication, a skill that served him well during court trials and negotiations. Opposing counsel actually moaned when they heard he was representing the opposite side. Yet here he sat, speechless and unsure of how to proceed in getting this man out of his house. As if reading the turmoil in his mind, the gentlemen leaned forward and placed his hand on Ron's knee. Immediately, Ron's muscles came alive, and he felt a peace that surpassed all understanding. He looked directly into the man's eyes and found there the sensation of complete trust. His mind cleared; however, his surroundings blurred. He knew where he was, everything was familiar. He could hear the grandfather clock ticking in the hallway; he recognized a cough from one of the upstairs bedrooms; and yet he felt like he was in a trance, existing within his body and outside his body at the same time.

The Holy Spirit was sitting in his easy chair, in his living room, in his home. *Yeah, right.* But each time he looked into those eyes and felt that peace, he knew it to be true. Finally, his mind changed gears. *How do you host the Holy Spirit? Do you offer him coffee? Is he tired? Would he like to freshen up? Who sets the agenda? What IS the agenda? Holy Smokes! Wait. That expression didn't seem appropriate, considering the presence of true holiness.* His mind whizzed back to all the times he had prayed that phrase, "Holy Spirit, I invite you to come more fully into my life." He meant it. Well, he thought he meant it, but surely not like this!

"Yes," his guest said, "I would like a cup of coffee."

Really? Ron did not remember saying that out loud, but he found himself in the kitchen retrieving a mug from the cabinet and pouring the hot brew. He couldn't remember how he got to the kitchen but he was there all right. This surreal feeling was making him feel dizzy.

"Cream? Sugar?" he called out. He set the mug down on the counter before his guest could respond and began laughing hysterically. Did he just ask the Holy Spirit if he wanted cream or sugar in his coffee? Wiping the tears from his eyes, he looked up and saw his guest standing in the doorway, still with that grin in his eyes and on his lips, filling up his whole face.

"Both, please."

Both, please. My guest, the Holy Spirit, will have both please. I will comply, and then I will go lie down in my bed. When I wake up again, I will share this ultimate crazy dream with my wife.

"Why don't we go into your den where we can sit and talk," the Holy Spirit suggested.

Okay, yes. Ron nodded. *Let's do that. Let's go into my den and have a talk, except when we get there, I am going to let you enter first and then slam the door shut behind you. When I open it again, you will not be there, and I will not have to commit myself to an asylum.* Then he did just that. Once the door was slammed, he sank to the floor and waited. He knew if he pinched himself, he would know for sure if he was dreaming. So he pinched himself. "*Ouch!*" he cried out.

Okay, enough pinching. Enough hysterics. He was a sane, intelligent man. Therefore, he knew when he opened the den door, the only thing to greet him would be his warm fireplace and his own, now cold cup of coffee. He wasn't timid about it. He threw open the door and rushed into the room. There, sitting in an easy chair by the fire was the Holy Spirit. He was sipping from his coffee mug and looking right at home. Ron's shoulders sagged. He walked over to the ottoman and plopped down beside him. "What? What is all this?" he asked.

"You called for me, and I came."

Ron stared at him intently. "Is this a habit of yours…to appear to people out of the blue and make yourself known this way? I have not once heard of such a thing ever happening. Why me?"

"When you seek me with all your heart, you will find me." He said it with such calm. It was his choice, and he chose to do it. End of topic.

Ron remained flabbergasted but decided the least he could do was take advantage of this situation. He did, after all, have questions. Why not get clarification on a few matters while he had His every attention. "Well, thank you," he said. That sounded lamer than he intended. "No, really, thank you for coming. Please forgive me. I am at a loss for words, let alone coherent thinking." The Holy Spirit just smiled. "Okay, here's the thing. There is something missing and I don't know what it is. You know I believe in you, in Father God, and in Son Jesus. I do believe in the Holy Trinity. I have accepted you all into my heart and life. So what's missing? Why do I still feel an ache for more?"

"Where is the ache?"

"What?"

"Where is this ache of yours? Is it in your heart, your mind, or your body?"

"Well," Ron contemplated, "all three, I guess. Maybe my heart, the most."

"Well then," replied the Holy Spirit as he set his coffee mug down on the end table, "let's take a look inside your heart."

Without any warning, Ron found himself deep within the chambers of his own beating heart. It glowed in pinks and reds with threads of blue crisscrossing in and out of the soft, pulsating mass. The Holy Spirit held tightly to his hand as they proceeded to the entrance of a room covered with a fine, spiderweb-like film.

"Enter," the Holy Spirit instructed as he gave him a gentle push through a slit in the doorway.

Ron waited for his eyes to adjust to the almost eerie dimness. He looked behind him, but the Holy Spirit had not followed. Turning back into the room, he saw an enormous flat-screen TV slowly encompassing the room until all the walls, the ceiling, and the floor were covered. Images began to appear. Images he didn't want to see just now. He immediately bristled. *How dare He!* This was his private room. He was the only one who knew about it. The pornographic images became more graphic as they flashed before his eyes. He sank to his knees. He covered his eyes and cried out but it did not stop the images from filtering through. *Why is He doing this?* He suddenly felt utterly alone and dejected. Then he became indignant again. *This was nobody's business. Not even his guest. Private matters should remain just that—private.* His wife didn't know this room existed. He never joined in with sexual innuendoes shared among his partners at the office so they had no reason to suspect he owned such a room. And his pastor...well, his pastor would be mortified.

The room had become suffocating. He felt like he couldn't breathe. The images kept flashing. He couldn't get away from them. He got up and stumbled around, looking for the doorway. There was none, just a mass of pulsating membrane around the room. He sank to his knees again and cried out. He had always known this was blatant sin. He knew it now but somehow it had gotten a hold on him. The more he fought it, the stronger the hold became. He was a slave to its enticement. He had never really wanted it in his life but was uncontrollably drawn to it like a magnet. Suddenly, he was so very ashamed. What was he thinking? Professing Christianity and living up to spiritual standards as far as the world knew but keeping this dark secret depravity.

He realized the room was becoming smaller, folding in on him as if to smother him. Tears began to roll down his face. He knew he was getting what he deserved, a recompense for all this wickedness. His face became contorted with sobs as he waited for the end. "I am so, so sorry. Please forgive me!" he wailed.

He felt a strong pulling force on his back. Abruptly, he popped out of the room and landed at the feet of the Holy Spirit. Still panting and sobbing, he looked up at those clear blue eyes. Saying he was deeply sorry again didn't seem to be required. Instead, he knelt before the Holy Spirit in total submission and humbleness. The Holy Spirit reached down and touched his shoulder, sending forgiveness and agape love into his entire being.

"Why did you make me go in there alone? It was almost more than I could bear."

"There was no room for me."

That statement awakened his understanding and brought instant clarification. Of course there wasn't. All these years, he had been asking the Holy Spirit to come more fully into his life…just not into this thought or that action and especially not *that* particular room. Other than those restrictions, he asked to "please come more fully." He almost wanted to laugh at how embarrassing this was and at how foolish he felt. The Holy Spirit reached down and pulled him to his feet. The same grin was on his face, filled with compassion.

The only thing Ron could say was, "I understand."

*   *   *

He shot straight up in bed, drenched in sweat. He was trying to grasp where he was. He looked to the other side of the bed. His wife was not there. *This must be what a heart attack feels like*, he thought. He eased back down onto the bed and tried to catch his breath. He heard kitchen noises and wonderful, familiar laughter coming from downstairs. It had been a dream, a wonderful, terrible dream. Could he remember all of it? Did he even want to?

The bedroom door opened a sliver, and his wife peeked in. "Hey, lazybones! You're finally awake. I thought you were going to sleep all day!"

"What time is it?"

"Eleven forty-five."

"What!" He sat straight up in bed again. "Are you sure?"

She laughed, "Yes, I'm sure. I just didn't have the heart to wake you. You seemed like you were off in another dimension. You were sleeping so soundly."

Yeah, he thought. *Maybe I was. But it's over now. Thank goodness it was just a dream.* A dream he would keep to himself, along with his fresh understanding. His sin had been dealt with, and he felt new. The chambers of his heart felt clean. He was ready to truly ask the Holy Spirit to come into his life—all of his life. No more picking and choosing. What a glorious realization.

He laid back down on the pillow and whispered, "Thank you for this insightful dream, Holy Spirit. Thank you for your cleansing power."

"Oh, by the way," said his wife, "I found this green satchel down in the living room. Is it something from work?"

*   *   *

For the sinful nature desires what is contrary to the Spirit, and the Spirit what is contrary to the sinful nature. They are in conflict with each other, so that you do not do what you want.
—Galatians 5:16–17 (NIV)

The Garden

The garden shimmered in sunlight, filtering through the dew-drenched leaves of the majestic oak trees. As far as the eye could see, moss-covered banks swooped low and soared heavenward in an uninterrupted waltz of emerald green. The scent of the garden continually radiated the washed-clean fragrance after a rain. Whiffs of lilac, lilies, roses, and heather all blended together, creating its own distinct aroma. There was a stillness in the garden but never silence. The songs of the whippoorwill and lark resonated loud and clear above the chittering of other small birds as they flitted from branch to branch warbling in unending joy. There was a perpetually calming peace in the garden. The sunlight seemed to float on the surface of the ponds, giving the lily pads a translucent effect. The greens of the garden were so deep; the yellows so delicate. The trees all grew strong and towering. The miracle of the garden? There were no weeds, only lush beauty.

One sound was out of place—the sound of quiet weeping. Mariah sat on a mound of grass, hands clasped about her knees as she swayed slightly to and fro in her misery and watched the gentle breeze ripple across the pond. Where was that sound coming from? Her lips were not parted and her eyes were not wet with tears. Still, she was surrounded with the sound of misery. She had been like this for less than a moment, but in that infinitesimal amount of time, the whole garden ceased to be. All movement, all color, and all light disappeared. Mariah shivered and knew she was in a lot of trouble. Of all the places in heaven, the garden was the most perfect and beautiful. No misery of any kind was ever allowed in the garden. Mariah tried to shrink into herself and waited.

"Mariah?"

"Yes, Lord?"

"You were in my garden."

"Yes, Lord."

"But you took misery in with you."

Mariah looked up and saw his presence. "Yes, Lord. I didn't mean to. I just entered for a moment's peace."

"Mariah, you know you are always welcome in the garden but not with misery. Misery is not allowed here."

Mariah frowned. Misery was not allowed anyplace in heaven, especially not for humans. Sometimes Mariah wished with all her might that she had been created as a human instead of an angel. Once in heaven, the humans faced nothing but moment after moment of joy and peace. She, on the other hand, had to constantly deal with the garbage of sin-filled lives.

The Lord knew Mariah's thoughts. "The humans had their share of suffering and misery on earth, Mariah. You know that. There is none for them here—ever."

"I know, Lord. I'm sorry." Mariah was humbled.

"Isn't your duty on earth?"

"Yes, Lord."

"Why then were you in my garden?"

How could she explain that she just sneaked away for one brief moment of refreshment? Mariah sighed. She didn't have to explain. He knew everything. "Oh Lord, couldn't I be taken off earth duty and be put into praise this eon? I am not doing a very good job, I'm afraid." The Lord smiled at Mariah. Mariah felt the warmth of His smile surround her. "Lord, you don't understand," she blurted out before she realized the absurdity of that statement. "Do you have any idea what my human is doing?" Mariah blushed. Sometimes she wanted to really overstep her bounds and demand to know how he could continue to love and forgive not just her human, who was totally immersed in self-destruction and sin, but the entire human race.

"She needs you, Mariah. You are the right arm of my Holy Spirit. Without your presence, she has no conscience at all. In these few seconds you have been absent from her, her heart is turning as cold as stone. You must go back immediately and touch that heart before it hardens. If that happens, I will lose her forever."

Mariah gasped as she jumped up, "Oh Lord, I don't want that! I am so sorry, Lord. I was just terribly disheartened for a while. She is so stubborn and, Lord, I think she is getting calloused."

"You must never give up. You must quietly coax and prod and sooth."

Mariah hung her head. "I will, Lord. But it is hard sometimes." Mariah wondered how her Lord could stand to look down upon all the sorrow and pain of his creation, how he could tolerate the injustices and sinful natures.

"Next time, Mariah, come to me. I will give you a strength blessing. The joy of my garden must never be interfered with, not even for one second."

Mariah felt even more miserable by her disobedience, knowing the garden was the most sacred of all places and still taking misery into it. She committed this atrocity before she even thought, and she was an angel. How much harder it must be for the humans. Mariah paused in her thoughts. *The Lord knows that. Well, of course He does. I am the one who forgot. The Lord let me feel this on purpose. He knew*

I needed to understand. Mariah looked up. "I understand, Lord." But the Lord was gone. The garden was gone.

She caught a glimpse of her human just coming out of the Cracker Box Lounge, hopelessly drunk again. Mariah floated to her side.

"Someday," she whispered as she gently pushed her out of the way of an oncoming car, "I'm going to take you for a walk in the most beautiful garden you can imagine."

*   *   *

> For he will command his angels concerning you to guard
> you in all your ways; they will lift you up in their hands,
> so that you will not strike your foot against a stone.
> —Psalm 91:11–12 (NIV)

Odessa

It was a quiet farming community. The only way to reach it without traveling the back dirt roads was to leave the freeway, follow Route 12, and wind your way through acres and acres of wheat fields. Just before harvest, if you were a stranger to the area, you could almost lose your bearings while driving through the maze of ripened grain. The motion of the golden stalks swaying in the wind was hypnotizing. There were no landmarks, no homesteads, and no intersecting roads; only miles and miles of gold performing a slow waltz with nature. Each curve in the road led to more of the same. After the first five miles, it was easy to imagine that you made a wrong turn along the way. But, since this was the only direct route to the town you knew that was not possible.

Eight miles further on, green, pointed spikes pierced their way into the horizon—poplar trees with only their very tops exposed. Suddenly, there it was, a drowsy little town nestled within a lush and protected hollow. On a grassy knoll just before descending down the steep, winding road that eventually became Main Street, there was a proud wooden sign that declared, "Odessa, established in 1885. Population, 625." It had been freshly painted.

It was a good town filled with good people. Although urban blight tried several times to inch its way into the citizenry of Odessa, it was always dealt a fatal blow. As the Mennonite pastor liked to remind everyone, "The Spirit that lives within us is far greater than the spirit within the world." Everyone always nodded when they heard that statement. It had become the unofficial town mantra. Odessa was a proud town, a close-knit town. Everyone watched out for everyone else. An old-fashioned barn raising? They were still done in Odessa. Potlucks? Every Saturday night along with square dancing at Pete and Melba's place just north of the outskirts of town. Generations of families, a great majority from German descent, lived and died in Odessa. The torch of kinship was successfully passed down to each new generation, and each new generation gladly accepted it. Community was well defined in Odessa.

Odessa didn't get many visitors. Those who joined in Thanksgiving and Christmas celebrations lived only a stone's throw away. Those few who did come in from farther away had visited for so many years that people didn't give them a second thought. The only regulars to come down the hill were the United Grocers truck every Thursday and an occasional UPS delivery van. United Grocers kept the one and only grocery store stocked with items that the locals couldn't grow or produce themselves. This included beer and wine for Jake's Bar & Grill. No hard liquor was allowed in the city limits even though the city limits had never been formally defined. If you wanted hard liquor, you had to take the forty-five-minute trip in to Danville and buy it yourself.

The heart of town consisted of two blocks. Doc Harwood was one of the first businesses to hang a shingle but most of his practice was done making house calls. Ada's Café served breakfast and lunch and had the best apple pie in four counties. The post office was a four-foot-long counter at the back of Odessa Mercantile. Except for the church, it was the oldest building in town and was still run by the Hiebert family. When they weren't selling flour and salt or various other sundries from the grocery shelves, Fritz and Gertie Hiebert took turns selling stamps and collecting letters and packages for mailing. They shared the title of postmaster, and every Tuesday, they also shared the duties of driving into Colfax to deposit the mail at the main county post office. They brought back with them a week's worth of mail and packages for the entire community. This weekly event didn't create a hardship for the town. People were accustomed to it. Getting mail once a week was the norm. Odessa City Hall was a one-room operation within the Mennonite church. Election of a mayor was done every two years by a show of hands at the end of services. The rotation was such that most of the men in town held the honor at least twice during their lifetime. Not much was involved in running the town. The town basically ran itself. Except for high school sports, there was no competition because there was only one of everything.

The only other building was the school. It was referred to as Odessa District School because half of the bottom floor was for elementary students, the rest of that floor and the entire second floor housed junior high, and the top floor was for high school. In 1956, the entire student body consisted of 103 pupils; eighteen were on the roster to graduate. Even though the Odessa Bulldogs had the least number of basketball players in the district, there was always enough to make a full team. They were a force to be reckoned with each year and held the respect of other schools. No one took time to analyze why but somewhere in the gut of the matter, the parents knew hard farm labor, strong spiritual values, and the unshakeable foundation of acceptance gave not just the team, but all the students a confidence that was hard to undermine. Like all schools, there was always a special clique, even though the small town camaraderie extended to everyone.

There was something special and extraordinary about a certain group of six on the roster to graduate that year. They were looked upon as the cream of the crop, the brightest, the best-looking, and the most energetic and focused at keeping their community the best it could be. The town couldn't have been prouder. The unbreakable bond between the six had solidified from the first day they took those tall, wide steps into the bus that would begin their scholastic adventure. They pretty much did everything together: learning their Bible verses in Sunday School, singing the opening hymn in front of the church congregation once a month, studying for tests, riding their horses on day-long adventures, and picnicking down at the old swimming hole summer after summer. As a general rule, if you saw one of them out and about, you saw all six. It only took until fifth grade for them to earn the moniker "The Six Pack."

Josh and Ellie were the main players of the group and your typical "sports hero goes steady with the prettiest cheerleader" duo. Everyone in the county knew they would eventually get married—or at least, they assumed they would. Ellie's folks owned the largest farm in the area. Their ninety-head of cattle required a lot of hay. The routine of running such a big enterprise (exclusive of shut-eye) was a 24-7, year-round endeavor. Extracurricular activities depended on getting the chores done first. Luckily, Ellie had four older brothers so she was free to come and go within a less stringent schedule.

Josh existed in an unsolicited aura of male perfection. He had the moxie to be the best. He was a man's man thanks to his dad, a lady's man based on the admiration he had for his mom. He was sensitive to women. Due to the fact that he loved and respected his mother so much, it came natural. She demanded gently; she loved passionately. He couldn't remember a time when she had not smiled every time she looked at him. Even well-deserved disciplinary action always ended with an enveloping hug. Through actions and attitudes, she taught him well about women just as his dad taught him well the nuances of being a man. He and his father were the center of his mom's universe, and she told them more than once she would step in front of a speeding bullet for them. She wasn't, however, a typical hausfrau. She was fiercely independent. Whenever it infringed on her time, her response had always been the same when his dad spouted, "JJ, we have to get out there and get the chores done before it gets dark." Her reply defined exactly who she was. "You got a mouse in your pocket?" Off he would go, feigning disgust in having to do the chores without her. Later, when she emerged from her bubble bath glowing and relaxed, he always came in to find his favorite meal waiting on the kitchen table. They didn't have to exchange words. The looks across the table said it all. Josh vowed that he would grow up to be just like them. Unconditional love, passion, respect, joy, and laughter—he would accept no less. He had found it in Ellie on the first grade bus. He didn't know love then, let alone passion. But, when she was sick or missed the bus, it was like his right arm had been severed. He was incomplete without her. She was as much a part of his being as a major internal organ. Yes, the assumption that he would marry and continue the family name with her was right on the mark. After college, they would marry and move to the old homestead and give his parents two or three dozen grandkids. Together his parents produced an unaffected, wise, and solid human being. If he had any regrets, it was that he and his dad had never once said "I love you" out loud. There were plenty of pat-on-the-back hugs but no verbal affirmations. They knew they loved each other deeply, but the words were never spoken.

Ellie, on the other hand, took nothing for granted. She needed to hear the words. Words, having a life of their own, took on greater power. Verbal affirmations helped solidify that others identified her the way she identified herself. Yes, she knew she was a knockout but it lost some of its luster without those verbal reminders. She didn't mean to be insecure. In fact, she hated it. Although she exuded confidence and pep and good cheer, that little ugly head of insecurity would pop up at the most inopportune times. She was not naïve to the looks and flirtatious advances other girls poured Josh's way. She was always relieved when he seemed to shrug them off. But it still upset her equilibrium. Sometimes she was absolutely positive they had become one even before the foundations of the earth. Other times, her mind spun with misgivings. Josh never gave her reason to doubt, but there was always the ill-conceived threat that someone from another school who was smarter, prettier, and more sophisticated would steal him away. Even though the townsfolk, usually led by her dad, talked like she was going to be a rock-solid pillar of the community someday and really make things happen while keeping them the same, all she really wanted was to be Josh's wife.

John was the quietest of the bunch. He was always getting ribbed for being a dreamer. His dreams had an intensity to them that humbled everyone when those thoughts became words on paper. He had a way with the written word. He always got an A-plus on his essays. Maybe he got it from his dad who was the Mennonite minister. Along with his mom and three little sisters, many hours were spent in Bible study and learning how to pray. He was debating about becoming an author or follow in his father's footsteps and become a minister. He loved the poetry of David in the book of Psalms and tried to copy Paul's way of getting his point across in Romans. Maybe in time, he would have the skill to do both. He definitely had the passion.

Mark was the rebel. Rules were meant to be broken as long as it didn't hurt anyone. Although Mark was a passenger on that first bus ride, he had pretty much kept to himself during those first three years of elementary school. It wasn't until the beginning of the fourth grade that it became clear to everyone why he shied away from the spotlight. Mark was an only child. He lived the farthest out on the bus route with his mom and dad in a small cabin partially hidden within a framework of pine trees.

One day, someone mentioned in Jake's Bar & Grill that they hadn't seen Mark's mom Olivia around town for a while. That piqued everyone's curiosity, and they began asking around. Hattie Schubert—who, years before, had crowned herself queen of all things suspicious—decided to make a house call. When she arrived at the ramble shack dwelling, she was told none too pleasantly by Mark's dad Jed that, although it was none of her business, Olivia had left them. The real story came out a few days later when Mark got on the bus with a black eye and a limp. The rest of the group insisted that he spill the beans and would not tolerate his aloofness one more day. With much coaxing, he finally shared that his dad had been abusive toward him and his mom for as long as he could remember.

One morning just before sunrise, she came into his bedroom, put her finger to her lips to signal his silence, and motioned for him to get dressed. They crept out of the house and into the nearest corn-field where their path would not be as detectable. It took most of the day but they walked and ran through field after field of corn and wheat all the way into Walla Walla. Mark was getting tired and hungry, but Olivia urged him on, telling him they didn't have time to stop. They could eat the sparse lunch she had packed back home once they got on the bus. When they arrived at the bus depot, she plunked down the money she had been storing away in a tin can under the porch and bought two one-way tickets to Henderson. All would have gone well if the bus had been on time. They both froze in place when they saw a cloud of dust looming in the distance. Olivia grabbed John's hand and ran around the side of the depot, looking for a place to hide. But it was too late, Jed had spotted them. He roared into the parking lot in his old '49 Ford pickup and didn't even bother to shut off the engine. Instead, he jumped out of the moving truck, letting it roll into and lodge against a tree at the edge of the property. He jerked Mark out of his mother's grasp and informed her that he was his son and that she could go to hell as far as he was concerned. If she ever came back and tried to snatch him away, he would kill her. With that, he marched Mark to the pickup and nearly threw him inside. Olivia was left drowning in her sobs, too frightened to react. Mark watched in terror through the grime-covered back window as she disappeared into the distance. The truth spread like wildfire, and with the whole town up in arms, a good old-fashioned vigilante formed within the hour. Jed was run out of town and told he was the one who would meet an untimely death if he ever showed his face again. Mark was immediately welcomed with open arms into Josh's family. Josh couldn't have been happier as he was an only child too. From a friendship that was already firmly established, it didn't take long for them to become as close as real brothers. Jed was never heard from again. The town was back to normal. The cyst had been forcibly removed before it could fester and spread its evil puss any farther. To this day, no one knows what became of Olivia.

Sara and Nadine were like two peas in a pod. Both had auburn hair and hazel-colored eyes. They were the same size and spent so much time borrowing each other's clothes that no one could tell by looking in their closets whose was whose. They had the same taste in food and music and just about everything else. Toward the end of their junior year, they spent hours and hours making after-graduation plans. Sara's folks owned the grocery store and planned for her and her younger brother to take the reins someday. The thought of it made her blanch. She wanted to live in the outside world. Everyone and everything in Odessa seemed so isolated from the allure of those other places. It wasn't that the town was ignorant to the outside world. After having watched *The Ed Sullivan Show* in disbelief as a crazed singer swung his hips in a most appalling and suggestive manner, the parents of Odessa had many nervous conversations about the next generation of outsiders going to hell in a handbasket. They were also on the alert for a new threat in the form of a cigarette called marijuana. This, in itself, was the biggest problem for Sara. She didn't want to just hear about these things, she wanted to experience them. The small, uneventful town of Odessa was too confining for her. She wasn't sure yet how she would tell her parents that when she went away to college, she would not be coming back. Maybe she would just get there first and then write them a letter.

Nadine pretended to agree with Sara but she was much less confident. She chilled from the idea that they might be drifting apart, that this pea-pod friendship might change, that it might not go on forever within the same status quo. Nadine liked her town. She liked the comfortable sameness about it. Everyone was so dependable; everyone was so protective. Look at what they'd done to Mark's father. She liked that shield of safety. She liked her home and her parents who had been surprised by the late-in-life pregnancy. Her three sisters were already in high school when she was born. Now they were all married and settled down with babies of their own on farms within the surrounding community. The outside world didn't hold the same adventurous allure to her as it did for Sara. It wasn't that she wanted to negate the idea of leaving. She really could do that as long as she did it with Sara. Someone would have to be the dependable and self-assured one in this venture, and it sure wouldn't be her. Her dreams of the future, however, didn't include never coming back. It was in her heart and her genes to come back someday, get married, and raise a happy family just like her sisters. That sounded more ideal than an ongoing adventure in a dangerous, unknown world.

The worst thing that can happen within the pendulum of time is to take self-expression for granted. Sara was pushing the envelope. She had suddenly become more aggressive within her experimental stage.

It was a lazy spring Saturday, and the six had just finished roping out into the old swimming hole. There were no cares as they lazed around on the mossy embankment. Graduation was just weeks away.

"Why can't we try marijuana?"

"Why do I have to save my virginity for marriage?"

The rest of the group was dumbfounded. If anyone would have taken that first sexual step, it would have been Josh and Ellie. Josh, however, had that deeply ingrained respect factor going for him, and Ellie was actually relieved that she could depend on him for those types of decisions. It had been close a few times but somehow, the brakes always skidded on. After Sara's comments, the eye-rolling that went around the group spoke volumes, but it was the shrugs that proved fatal. They all assumed it was just a stage she would outgrow in short order. No one realized that she was the pivot point to their future.

That next Tuesday, Ellie went downtown to retrieve the mail and buy new canning lids for the apricots her mother was preserving. As she walked past the small greenway in the middle of town, she saw Nadine sitting on the park bench crying. It was not unusual to see Nadine distraught, but she could not remember a time when she had seen her this dejected. Without a word, she walked over and put her arm around her shoulder. Maybe it was just the uncertainty of graduation and what came next. After several more sobs, Nadine took a deep breath and in one elongated sentence, spilled out that Sara had not only gone into Pullman the past weekend to try sex, she had also smoked marijuana. It was tearing Nadine's world apart. Sara was supposed to be her strength, her shelter in the big, bad world when they ventured out together. Now she couldn't trust her. Her world had come crashing down. After the initial shock, Ellie could only mutter something about what an idiot Sara was. That didn't help matters. Nadine burst out into new heart-wrenching sobs. Life had been in steps—step one, step two, step three. Everything in order; everything planned out. No one had forewarned Nadine that every so often, there would be a splinter in the staircase, that one plank might have rotted completely away, and when she stepped on it, down she would go. Suddenly, she didn't even want to think graduation, let alone what lay ahead. All Ellie could do was hug her more tightly and try to reassure her that everything would be okay. Her reassurances came out rather lame because this revelation had spun her world off-kilter too.

It was time for a group meeting sans Sara. They met down at the swimming hole. There under the large branch-laden overhang of a solid hundred-year-old oak tree, Ellie related the problem with Nadine filling in a few blanks. Everyone was silent for a while.

Finally, John spoke up and shocked the rest of the group beyond belief. "So what's wrong with that?"

They all looked at him, dumbfounded. *Didn't he get it? Didn't he understand that they had goals to accomplish without bringing the garbage of the world into play? And he wanted to be a minister! Of them all, he should have been the most appalled.*

"Listen up, guys. I've been thinking a lot about our futures too." John gestured while pacing back and forth on the sand. "We think Odessa is the center of the universe. We think we've got the world by the tail. There isn't anything that we can't tackle and deal with. All I'm saying is, maybe we can, maybe we can't. But how are we supposed to know if we don't meet stuff head-on and make our own decisions through experience?"

"What good am I going to be to your kids as a minister"—he nodded at Josh and Ellie—"if I don't have a clue what they're into and how I can direct them away from it? I, for one, have thought a lot about this smoking thing. What's the harm? I've heard that it only brings on peace and a sense of contentment. Who wouldn't want that?"

The rest of the group sat, still dumbfounded, and stared at him. Was this really their John Boy, the solid, deep-thinker of the group? They assumed that in that deep thinking, he analyzed everything to the nth degree and came up with the right answer every single time.

Mark responded first. "I've had sex."

Ellie jumped to her feet. "What? You've had sex, Sara has had sex. Am I the only one in the universe who hasn't had sex?"

Josh grinned at her. "I haven't." Ellie rolled her eyes and refused to think about their make-out sessions that pretty much included everything but consummation.

In the same breath, both John and Josh asked Mark, "When?"

Mark blushed and said, "I'll tell you later."

Nadine was in tears again. John went to her side and gave her a big back-rubbing hug. "It's time to grow up, Nadine."

At that, everyone was silent again. They had been so eager to reach this stage of being an adult. It suddenly seemed more than daunting.

"WHAT?" someone yelled from the top of the hill. Everyone turned around in time to see Sara clomping down the slope. "Since when am I not a part of this group? Did we call a meeting to vote me out?" Her face was beet red when she reached the bottom of the hill and stood confrontationally in the center of the group. She turned and eyed each of them individually. "What?" she said again.

Josh got up and took her arm, leading her to the large rock on which years ago he had etched "Josh and Ellie" within a big heart. Sara sat down. "Actually, Sara, we were talking about you. We were admiring your fearlessness." Ellie gave him a funny look. He acknowledged the question in her eyes and continued, "We've been best buds since first grade. We've partied together, we've laughed together, and we've bonded in the most adverse of circumstances." With this, Josh looked directly at Mark to make sure he caught the significance. "I don't like the idea that within days we are all going our separate ways. Sure, we have telephones and yes we will see each other during the holidays. But nothing is going to be the same. Basically, we're out of here. Once we all get to college, we're going to be like an octopus, still connected but with tentacles going all different directions. Honestly, Sara, I think we're all a bit jealous that you were the first to spread your wings and try new things, things we have made it a point to avoid. When all is said and done, you turned out to be the leader into our future. What more can I say?"

Sara liked what she was hearing and relaxed her shoulders. She let out the breath she had been holding. Then she looked directly at Nadine. "So you spilled the beans, huh?" Nadine nodded slightly. "So okay, the cat's out of the bag. Your sweet Sara is no longer a virgin. But don't for a minute think that marijuana was the culprit. They happened at two separate times. They were both amazing. And I plan to do them both again and again and a whole lot more." The uncertainty within the group as to where to go from here was almost palatable.

Finally, Mark ventured out to say, "So how was it?"

"Which one?" Sara smiled slyly.

"Both."

Sara got up, plopped down on the grass beside Mark, and looked deep into his eyes. "What can I say, Mark? They were both exciting. There is no other word to describe either of them. Marijuana is amazing, such peace. All Stresses just melted away and I couldn't stop giggling."

"Where did you get it?" Josh asked.

"From someone I met at a basketball game in Pullman."

"Could you get more?" Josh continued.

"What?" Ellie shouted. This couldn't be the Josh who one day would be the father of her children.

Josh left Sara's side and went to Ellie. "Don' slip a disk, El. I was just asking."

"Sure, I can get more. Anytime you want. In fact, I think that would be a great way to celebrate graduation, celebrate us, and bond one last time in a private ritual that we could store up for a grand memory in our old age."

"It's a thought," Josh replied. Ellie slugged him on the shoulder.

John stood up and started pacing. "Is it addictive?"

"No."

"How do you know that?"

"That's what everyone has told me. Besides, I don't have a craving to do it again."

"How much will it cost?"

At this, Ellie jumped to her feet, put her hands on her hips, and shouted at no one in particular, "What are you thinking? Number one, it is illegal. Number two, we can't take *everyone's* word that it isn't addictive. Number three…well, number three is we shouldn't be doing stuff like that."

"Why not?" Mark shrugged.

"It's not who we are," Nadine whispered.

Everyone looked at Nadine and was somehow able to project her into the future of herself—fearful, hesitant, and scared of her own shadow. It was that unified look of understanding that changed the whole tone of the group. No one, not even Ellie, wanted to grow into that kind of person. What was life all about without some adventure and experimentation? How else would you really know life?

John stopped pacing. "I love you guys, you know that. You've been my life's blood for twelve years now. I say we do this thing. We do it together. We support the hesitant and give ourselves one final hoorah before graduation. If we're in it together, what harm could it do just once?"

"I agree," chimed in Mark. "It's now or never for me."

Josh noticed the smile spreading across Sara's face but he was more in tune to the scowl on Ellie's. He waited. He continued to watch her as she mentally processed the pros and cons. Although he might go out on his own and try this another time, he was not going to step into this group decision without her.

The ice broke when she asked, "Where would we do it? It shouldn't be close to home."

Nadine stood up and walked toward the water's edge. "I'm scared," was all she said.

In unison, the remaining five got up and went to her. "We know you're scared, Nadine, but we'd be in this together. One for all and all for one, that sort of thing," said Sara.

"Yeah," Mark said more boldly. "We do it as a group or we don't do it at all."

"I'm in," said Ellie.

Josh was pleased, if not a little shocked. He threw his arm around her. "Yeah, we're in!" he boasted.

"Make that five," John chorused.

The only holdout now was Nadine. She looked around the group and realized how much she loved them and how much she depended on them all these years. She was going to have to commit right now or she would turn into a blubbering pile of mush. "Okay, me too."

Sara said she would make the buy. They decided to meet early at Josh's house the following Friday night and drive over to the district championship game at Steptoe Butte together. Josh said he would get the coach's okay to travel in a private vehicle rather than with the team on the bus. Sara made good on the buy, and by five that Friday evening, they were all gathered at Josh's to start the trip. If they seemed a little more anxious than usual, Josh's folks just chalked it up to the big game. The Bulldogs were favored to win and then off to state once again. The plan was to drive back down to the river, do the deed, and then continue on to the game. Everyone was in good spirits and excited to take that first puff. Although Sara had only experimented once, they still deferred to her as the expert.

"Plan to feel a little lightheaded at first then this crazy peace will take over, and you won't have a care in the world."

She lit up and took the first hit. She closed her eyes and handed it off to Mark. Mark followed suit and handed off to John. He didn't inhale quite as deeply but he paid attention to the ritual and closed his eyes too, hoping to feel awe as this new door opened up to him. Josh and Ellie took their turns and handed over to Nadine. You would have thought she was a user. In one swift motion, the joint was at her lips. She puffed in until her lungs felt like they would explode. She psyched herself beforehand that this was something she must do quickly or she would back out. With all six waiting to feel that certain something, the joint went back to Sara. Once again, she inhaled and passed it on. After it had been passed from hand to hand for the third time, there was nothing left to clench their lips around.

"Don't worry," Sara smiled. "I bought more. We can finish them on the way."

Everyone nodded with a seemingly profound understanding of that statement. Hugs were passed back and forth. Then through lazy smiles, they were suddenly all in tears, tears of remembrance and tears of solidarity. They all walked arm in arm to the car. It had started to rain. Josh drove with Ellie at his side. On her right was John. In the back, Mark sat between Sara and Nadine. The second joint was passed around. With each new puff, deeper serenity settled over them.

"Are you okay to drive," Ellie asked as she nestled her head on Josh's shoulder.

"Never been better," he replied with a sigh.

The rain began to pelt the car with a tin-ping rhythm. It was very soothing. Life was good. Conquering the world had never been so close to their fingertips. No one spoke for a very long time but drifted off into his or her own private memories of time spent within each friendship and all the times spent together.

Josh bent down and whispered into Ellie's ear, "I love you, you know."

She sighed and said, "Me too," as she reached up to kiss him on the ear.

The car must have hydroplaned on the wet surface. The only thing they would remember was skidding around and around in 360-degree turns and then slamming head-on into a large oak tree ten or twelve feet off the main road. The force was so violent that all six passengers were spit out of the mangled car onto the soggy ground. For a few moments, everyone was stunned.

Josh was the first to speak. "I'm sorry, I'm so sorry! Is everyone okay?"

One by one, they mumbled something to indicate that they were indeed okay.

"Except I'm pretty sure my leg is broken," groaned John.

Mark tried to sit up and howled in pain. "At least it's not your back!" he muttered between clenched teeth.

Josh called out for Ellie. She was already standing and brushing leaves and mucky sod from her skirt. "I'm fine, Josh. I'm okay."

Josh lay back down on the ground and began to sob. "I'm sorry. I'm so sorry!"

"It wasn't your fault, Josh," said Nadine in a very composed voice. "You weren't even speeding. It just happened. Look, we're all okay. Everything is going to be okay."

"Where's Sara?" Mark asked.

"Sara?" Ellie called, looking around the perimeter. No answer. 'Sara?" she called out again, more urgently.

"Here! I'm here," came a faint voice from under the back of the car.

Ellie was at her side in an instant. "Where does it hurt, Sara? Are you okay?"

"I'm okay. It doesn't hurt anyplace."

Ellie almost fainted when she saw the huge gash in her side. It looked like the top of her torso had been ripped wide open and was barely attached to the bottom. "Help! Someone help! She's going to bleed to death!" Ellie screamed.

Just then, bright lights appeared in the distance. Within seconds, a pristine white Mercedes van pulled alongside the wreckage site. A tall, marvelous woman emerged from the driver's side and surveyed the scene. She was the most amazing thing the boys had ever seen. Her golden hair hung down in loose folds below her shoulders. Her body was astonishingly lithe. Each boy had the same response to her. It was a staggering desire to cater to her every whim, and see to it that she never had a bad day. And yet, they somehow knew it was she who would be doing all that for them. They were flabbergasted by her beauty. The girls were in awe. When she smiled at each of them in turn, they knew they were seeing perfection. She was there to care for each of them. She exuded an aura of acceptance and true peace.

"What happened?" she said with a tone that implied she already knew.

John spoke, "I think we hydroplaned."

"Some things are better left unexplored," she said softly but matter-of-factly. They all caught the implication. How could she have known of their experiment? She had just arrived. No one responded. "Do any of you know Jesus?" she asked kindly. There was a stunned silence.

"I do," said Ellie.

"What do you know about Him?"

"Well, I know that He is the Son of God and I know that He is my Savior."

"That is very wise of you, Ellie. Why don't you come sit in the car and get your wits about you."

Ellie nodded numbly. With the beautiful lady's arm around her waist, she walked over to the car and slid into the middle seat of the Mercedes.

"Does anyone else here know Jesus?" she ventured again. Only silence. "Well, rest easy. Help is on the way." They all heard the distant sirens at the same time. The woman walked back to her car, closed Ellie's door, and got in behind the wheel. She turned the key in the ignition and smiled at Ellie in the rearview mirror. "Let's take a ride and get you together again."

As she pulled away from the accident scene, Ellie called out to her, "Wait, not without Josh! Look at him, I can see on his face that he wants to come too. You shocked him, that's all. You are so beautiful, I think you left him speechless. Please, can't we go back for him?"

"As you wish." She backed the car to the spot where Josh still lay.

Ellie's door opened automatically, and she called to him, "Josh, do you want to come too? Tell her you know Jesus. It seems to be the key."

Josh squinted up at Ellie with blood-caked eyes. "Sure, I know Jesus. You know I do. I accepted him as my Savior in fifth grade, remember?"

"That's wonderful, Josh," said the lady. "Why don't you get up and slide into the seat next to Ellie." Josh did what he was told.

'Wait!" hollered John. "I'm not sure of the significance of all this, but I'm a believer too. Is there room for me?"

The lady smiled more warmly than before and said softly, "There is room for anyone and everyone who is a true believer. Why don't you slip into the back seat, John. Anyone else want to come along?"

Nadine who had been sitting in a rather large mud puddle raised her hand. "I'd like to be with my friends please."

"That's not quite enough, dear. Now that you stop to think about it, do you have a very best friend?"

Nadine pondered that question and then her eyes lit up. "Yes! Yes, I do. Jesus has always been my very best friend. Ever since I accepted him as my Savior in junior high school, He helped me not to be so scared sometimes, and whenever I talk to Him, He makes things less frightening."

The lady opened the passenger door and motioned for Nadine to get in. Again, she accelerated and started down the road. In unison, the four called out, "Wait! Please! What about Mark? We can't go without Mark!"

The lady stopped the van once again and seemingly floated over the ground to Mark's side. Mark was in obvious pain. "Mark?" Mark covered his face with his mud-splattered hands. "Mark, do you want to go with us?"

"No, I'm not worthy."

"Who told you that, Mark?" Mark let out a sob. "Mark, it's okay. You can tell me."

Mark sobbed even harder and could barely spit out the words. "My dad."

"Mark, you must listen to me and believe me. That is a lie. Jesus loves you very much. He loves you so much that He died for you."

Mark wiped his shirt sleeve across his eyes. "Yeah, I heard that in Sunday school. But he wasn't thinking about me when he did that."

"Mark, are you trying to make me believe that Jesus died for everyone *but* you?"

Mark looked confused. That didn't quite compute. "Yes…no. Well, I don't know about everyone else but I'm pretty sure he didn't die just for me. Nobody could love me that much."

"Jesus does. He loves you more than you could ever imagine. You are one of his very special creation, and He doesn't want to lose you."

"What do you mean *lose me?*"

"If you don't believe in Him and what He did to save you, He has no option than to lose you to yourself and your own selfish fate. He wants you to be with Him forever. In fact, He has prepared a very special place just for you."

"Are my friends going to have a special place too?"

"Yes, dear. In fact, Jesus will see to it that you will all be neighbors. The only directive is that you truly believe in Him, His love, His death, and His resurrection for you."

"I do believe that, ma'am. I guess I always have. I just never gave it much thought."

She smiled. "Well, how about thinking it through right now and making a decision one way or the other."

Mark looked down and then directly back into her eyes. They were the clearest and most disarming blue he had ever encountered. "I do believe, ma'am. I believe all that Sunday school stuff. I want to be with my friends, and I want to be with Jesus. I've always needed someone to understand me."

"He does, Mark. He knows you inside out. Here, let me help you up so you can join us in the van. We have a quick trip to make and then you can rest."

The five of them sat in peaceful silence in the van, waiting for the beautiful lady to drive them to the next and final step in their lifelong journey. It was rather odd that no one thought about Sara. It was as if she had never been a part of them or never even existed. None of them had noticed when the beautiful lady first pulled up that she left the car and went to Sara's side with a sense of urgency. They talked. The beautiful lady invited Sara to join her in the van.

Sara grimaced. Somehow she knew this was very important but she wasn't about to give up her newfound freedom. The beautiful lady asked her if she knew Jesus. "Oh yes, absolutely," she responded.

"Absolutely *what?*"

"I know about Jesus."

"Sara, knowing *about* Him and knowing Him are entirely different." Sara didn't like where this conversation was headed. "Jesus would like you to come with us when we leave."

"I'd like to do that, I really would. But not now. There are several more things I want to see and experience first. Could I come later?"

"Sara, those things you seek all lead to death. Jesus is the only way, the truth, and the life. You need to decide right now."

Sara definitely didn't like being told that. This lady was starting to cramp her style. "Well, in that case, I think I'll wait awhile. I just met someone, and we're going to a party after the game."

"Sara, think carefully about your decision. This could be your last breath. There may not be time for that decision later."

Sara stretched up her arms and twirled them in the air. Then she stood up and said, "No, look, I'm fine, and there is some stuff I want to do first. I'm just beginning to realize how wonderful this world can be." She looked up at the beautiful lady who somehow seemed taller and more imposing. "I'd like to come with you, really I would. Could we talk about this later?"

The beautiful lady began to drift back to the van. "I'm so very, very sorry, Sara. I'm afraid you have already sealed your own fate." With those last words, Sara's spirit crumpled back into her body that was laying on the wet, cold ground. She took a last gasp of air.

Everyone in the van should have felt broken and exhausted. Instead, they were basking in the warmth of an all-encompassing peace. The trauma they had just gone through seemed surreal to them now, just out of reach from their current reality.

"Please rest now, precious children. You've had a traumatic afternoon. Rest in peace. We'll be home soon."

Ellie smiled as her head dipped toward her chest. She had no worries. Just before deep sleep, Josh was heard to say, "I love you, Dad."

Mark finally found peace and left all earthly cares behind him for the last time. Nadine was momentarily confused as to where all her fears had gone. Every fiber of her being was at rest. Her last, long sigh was filled with an everlasting serenity. John's last waking thought was filled with wonder but he couldn't quite form that wonder into a coherent thought. Then he too was sound asleep. None of them felt the van lift off the ground, saw the stars flash by in all their brilliance, or sensed the thrust as they time-warped into another dimension. When the van touched down, they all woke up instantly.

The beautiful lady turned in her seat. "Welcome to your new eternal home. It has been my pleasure to serve you."

They all tumbled out of the car at the same time, laughing and hugging and wondering about their new spiritual bodies. They were standing in front of a golden gate so wide and so high that you could not see the sides or the top of it.

Ellie tapped Josh on the shoulder, "Look!"

They all turned and watched in stunned amazement at the bright light moving toward them down the pathway toward the gate. The closer the light came, the more clearly they could detect a body. It was Jesus. When He got to the gate, it swung wide open. They looked around at each other in delight, and before anyone could speak, they found themselves running to Him.

He threw His head back and laughed with them and somehow hugged all of them at the same time. "I am so delighted to see all of you, my precious ones. I've been waiting for this day." They clung to Him and His every word for what seemed an eternity. Much too soon, He said kindly, "There are many more who want to greet you, and I have other matters to attend to. Please enter your new home. I bless you with continuous peace and harmony."

The most difficult thing they had ever done was break away from His embrace but they trusted what He said and bowed their heads in reverence. A few steps down the path, they could hear Him laughing again as He waved to a little girl running up the path toward him. Then as if out of the clouds, they were surrounded with joyful, applauding people.

Josh's grandfather scooped him off the ground, twirled him around and around, and said, "I'm so proud of you!"

Nadine was greeted by two charming little girls who looked exactly alike. "Hi, welcome!" they said in unison. Then they giggled, realizing she had no idea who they were. "We're your sisters! Twin sisters! We were only three weeks old when we traveled down the birth canal. Mom had a miscarriage that she didn't even know about."

Nadine thought she had died and gone to heaven. Wait, she had! She gathered them into her arms, and together they laughed and began the wonderful mission of getting to know each other.

Ellie was immediately surrounded by some of her loved ones: her favorite cousin who had been electrocuted by a downed power wire, another cousin who was only seventeen when he died in a head-on motorcycle accident, and several aunts and uncles. Still coming toward her for the celebration, she recognized her old Sunday school teacher. In fact, it was the lady who helped her give her heart to Jesus. It was overwhelming. There were so many waiting to greet her. The verbal affirmations never seemed to cease.

John didn't wait to be greeted. He was full speed ahead and ran right into the arms of his grandmother. They hugged and laughed for the longest time. Then he felt more bodies pressing against him and began to make out the faces of other friends and family members. He was trying in vain to process all this so he could get these feelings down on paper.

Then, as if on cue, everyone quieted down and shushed each other. They looked at Mark and waited.

"What?" he asked.

They all smiled but said nothing. Coming down the path was a strikingly beautiful woman. Her loving gaze toward Mark was enough to shatter evil. Mark peered at her. When she came into full focus, it took only one leap for him to land in her embrace. Olivia.

Everything was so overwhelmingly delightful. The ongoing joy was contagious. They all knew they would never stop smiling and laughing for the rest of eternity.

Back on planet earth, the town of Odessa would never be the same.

* * *

There is a way that seems right to a man,
but in the end it leads to death.
—Proverbs 16:25 (NIV)

Lydia

She sat straight as an arrow, her hands gripping the steering wheel so tightly that her knuckles turned white. Years ago, an old, frayed couch cushion had become a permanent fixture in her 1956 Studebaker, adding another six inches to her five-foot-two frame and allowing her to see comfortably through the windshield. She glanced frequently at the map spread out on the seat beside her and smiled every time she looked at the large circle drawn around the name Lancaster, her destination. For the seemingly hundredth time, she took one hand from the steering wheel and reached down, feeling in her skirt pocket to make sure the key was still there. It was. This wasn't just any key, this was the key to her future—a key she had been longing for ever since she had gotten her teaching certificate from the university.

The scenery became monotonous. There was nothing to see except an expanse of clear, blue sky and the long asphalt snake winding through fields of early fall wheat. According to her calculations, she would be arriving in another ten minutes, give or take. It was very convenient that the school was only twenty minutes from her trailer park in Push. Push. She had always thought it the craziest of names and often wondered how the town came to be. She researched it at the county hall of records and asked around, but the townspeople just shrugged and told her it had been that name for over a century, and no one seemed to know why. There wasn't much to the town. The population barely topped two hundred, thirty of whom lived in her trailer park.

The call came just three days before. She had been out in her six-by-six plot of garden, tending to the weeds that seemed to be growing faster than the vegetables. By the time she realized the phone was ringing, it took her some time to unwind from her kneeling position next to the tomato plants and climb the stairs into her trailer. She almost missed the call. "Hello?

"Ms. Spencer?"

"Speaking."

"This is Mr. Severson from the Lancaster Public School District. Do you have a moment?"

Lydia's heart skipped several beats, and she had to clear her throat before answering. "Yes. Yes, I have a moment, Mr. Severson."

"Very good, Ms. Spencer. I would like to advise you that we have a teaching position open in our district, and we are wondering if you might have time to interview this coming Thursday. We are a small district, and your skills would be required for the first- and second-grade classes, which are combined."

Lydia wanted to shriek into the receiver, "No interview necessary. I will take the job sight unseen. I don't care what the salary structure is, I accept." Instead, she calmed herself and replied, "Why, yes, Mr. Severson. I am available on Thursday and very interested in this position."

"Very good, Ms. Spencer. Very good. I will post a key to you in tomorrow's mail." He proceeded to give her directions.

Lydia had never been quite sure of herself or how she fit in the world. Nothing in her life seemed to click. She graduated from the university just over four years ago, and although she had interviewed a dozen or more times, the positions always went to someone "more qualified"—whatever that meant. Maybe because her education was focused on librarian skills, they assumed she didn't know how to teach. Goodness. If she could teach children how to use the Dewey Decimal System, she could surely teach them their ABCs. None of that mattered now. She had gotten the call. Funny, how you know when you know. This was not just another call, this was *the* call. She sensed it from her insides out. She became mesmerized during the final ten miles to her destination. There were no other cars on the road, and there was really no need to stay alert. She thought back to her not-so-distant past.

She was an only child, sired by the well-known town drunk in his elderly years. Her mother, being twenty-five years younger, decided to stick around because of the security. Pop's paychecks from the textile factory came like clockwork once a month. He may not have been generous with his person, but at the end of each month, he went to the bank, cashed his check, allotted a hundred dollars for his booze, and gave the rest to his wife for paying bills and taking care of the snot-nosed kid he had not wanted. As long as the bills got paid, he didn't give a hoot where else the money went. Just leave him the hell alone with his bottle and quit asking him to do things, go places, and all that other poppycock women are so apt to want.

Having ventured down memory lane, Lydia now had all kinds of thoughts whirling in her mind. She never liked the boys who were attracted to her. She wasn't even sure they were attracted. It was more like she was their last hope. They had no chance with the cheerleaders and even less chance with the intellectuals. The shy girls shied away; the aggressive girls snubbed their noses. Who did that leave? Lydia. She could never quite figure it out. She was definitely not drop-dead gorgeous, but then again, neither was she repulsive. No one could mistake her for Mensa material, but she was also not intellectually disabled. All in all, she gave herself a nice, hearty 5 on a scale from 1–10. Rather mediocre in all aspects but not tipping toward one extreme or the other. Why then could she not attract a nice, comfortable male companion instead of choices that tipped toward the bottom of her expectations?

Lydia sighed. Then she laughed out loud. Her college days had been a repeat of high school. There had been no interest from either direction. It didn't seem to be in the cards for her and men. She had come to terms with that. Although it was quite lonely at times, she was content to sit and wait. Wait for what, she was not sure. She mostly bided her time working at Woolworth's down the road in the bigger town of Patterson and loving her cat, Panda. In the summer, she tended her garden; in the winter, she played scrabble against herself next to the space heater. Thank goodness for her pop. He had insisted that her mom buy the eight-year-old trailer she lived in. Lydia was pretty sure it was not out of the generosity of his heart, he was just mortified to think she might move back in with them. She remembered that phone call well. She had hated to ask for the money and promised with her dying breath that she would pay them back. Her mom rested the receiver against her chest, but Lydia could still hear the conversation between her and pops.

"For crying out loud, Betty! Don't loan her the money, buy her a used trailer. You think I don't know about your private savings account down at the credit union? Buy the trailer, and I don't want to hear any more about it."

Lydia let out another loud and prolonged sigh as this teaching opportunity started to sink in. She knew without any doubt that finally, this was it! This was what she had been waiting for. Here at last, she smiled to herself, here at last.

The road began winding down a steep incline. Halfway down, she looked out the right window, and there it was. The school. Her school. Her future. She almost hyperventilated. It was old—no, not old, established. It was plopped down right in the middle of a valley, surrounded by low rolling mountains on no less than a two-acre plot.

The surroundings were in complete contrast from her drive through the flat, never-ending wheat fields. It was a three-story structure with a concrete facade that had faded with time into a pale yellow. In some places, she could see where chunks of plaster had fallen away, leaving cream-colored scars behind. It was like a regal queen who had lost her tiara, but Lydia could see right through all that to a time when it held court in all its splendor. She could visualize the children laughing and gently jabbing at each other as they clambered up the steps to the front entrance—and what an entrance it was. The fourteen-step stairway was like a royal train, swooping in a semicircle to each side and beckoning the children to come; come quickly. Up the stairs they would have climbed, laughing and poking at each other in fun, ready to learn the fundamentals. Sponges. She was sure they had all been like sponges, absorbing the knowledge that would so benefit them in their own futures. Now it was her time to teach and nurture and share knowledge with them.

She turned down a short but wide patch of gravel and parked within a few feet of the entrance. She glanced over her shoulder at the five boxes setting on the back seat. She came prepared. Gingerly, she got out of the car and smiled up at her school. The midday sun was casting a serene, apricot-colored glow on its exterior. She had never encountered such a warm and inviting welcome and wanted very much to curtsy in respect. She was a little surprised that hers was the only car in the lot. She glanced at her watch. She wasn't early. In fact, she was right on time. Maybe other cars were parked around back where she could not see them. Closing the car door very gently so as not to break the reverie, she reached into her skirt pocket and retrieved the key. Slowly she ascended the stairs to the ten-foot high, etched-glass doors. Cupping her hands around her eyes, she peered through the doors and down a twelve-foot-wide hallway. There were several doors on each side, all closed. It was very still. She wondered why the principal, at the very least, was not on the premises preparing for the school year. She tried the door latch. It was locked. Ever so reverently, she braced her left hand against the window pane and with a shaking right hand, slipped the key into the keyhole and turned the bolt to her future.

"Hello?"

Lydia walked somewhat timidly down the corridor. She now understood the sound of silence. She crisscrossed from side to side, opening each closed door and looking inside. All classrooms were empty except for the blackboards and school desks. *How odd*, she thought. *When would the other teachers start preparation for the school year?* The first day was fast approaching. Tuesday after Labor Day was right around the corner. She shook her head and continued down the hallway. When she opened the last room on the right, she felt it. She knew immediately this was to be her room, her domain. She entered and flipped on the light switch, its fluorescent buzz immediately filling the silence. It looked no different from the other classrooms with a blackboard and four rows of children's desks on wooden runners facing her desk at the front. *Her desk!* She wanted to shout it to the rafters.

Lydia walked over to the window and stared down at the weeds encroaching the gravel in the parking lot. Her car sat idle and alone. It reminded her of what she needed to do. Since no one was here yet for the interview, she might as well get started. Almost skipping, she raced back through the corridor and down the entrance steps. Reaching into the back seat of her car, she took out the five boxes, stacking them on the ground. Three trips later, they were all in her room, ready to be unpacked. She began immediately. Having found a stepladder in a janitor's closet down the hall, she began attaching a twelve-inch-high banner of ABCs above the blackboard. Then she emptied one box of supplies into the drawers of her desk. She placed two pieces of chalk and an eraser into the runner of the chalkboard, pulled out her jade plant, and placed it on the window sill. It needed water. The desks needed dusting. The floor needed sweeping. She became her own janitor, and by the time she was done, the room looked like classes had been held in it every day for the past year. Pleased as punch, she sat down at her desk, folded her hands, and surveyed her beloved kingdom. Finally, she was home. Life was starting to make sense.

"My, my, my! You don't waste any time, I see."

Lydia jumped at the sound of the voice. It was coming from the back of the room. How he had appeared so quietly, she didn't know, but there he stood, smiling at her. "Oh, my!" Was that all she could muster?

"Oh my, indeed," he replied as she watched him seemingly glide down the aisle toward her. He was still smiling. "I am Mr. Severson. I presume you are Ms. Spencer?"

Lydia's face reddened as she realized how presumptuous she had been. She looked around and her heart sank. What in the world had possessed her? How could she have marched into this school and taken over as if she owned the place when she hadn't even been offered a position yet? Clumsily, she stood from her chair, its wooden legs scrapping across the linoleum floor. "Oh, my," she repeated. "I do so apologize. I am afraid I have lost my senses. I am not sure what came over me. It's just…well, it just seemed to…" she hesitated. "Everything seemed to fall into place." She raised her eyebrows and cocked her head toward him in a sheepish manner that implied she was at a total loss to explain.

Mr. Severson threw his head back and let out a bellowing laugh that filled the entire room. "You are perfect, my dear. Absolutely perfect! More than I could have expected and more than I could have hoped for. No interview necessary. The job is yours if you will have it."

Lydia stared at him, dumbfounded and in disbelief. "Really?" was all that came out of her mouth.

"Really!" he responded with another roar of laughter.

Mr. Severson was tall. Quite tall, in fact. Lydia guessed him to be at least six foot three or more. It was amazing that he moved so gracefully. He was also quite thin; actually, gaunt was a better description. He wore a dark, navy suit and, the oddest thing, a tall stovepipe hat like the kind Abe Lincoln might have worn. Even though his laughter was jolly, it didn't quite reach his eyes. They seemed dull and expressionless.

"Please sit down, Ms. Spencer," he motioned with a sweep of his hands that extended from his long, apelike arms.

Lydia sat immediately and abruptly. She stared at him, expecting the anvil to fall. Yes, she heard him say the job was hers if she would like it but, under the circumstances, that could have merely been something said during an awkward encounter.

"I like what you have done with your room, very impressive. You have a knack for organization, I see. That will prove quite useful." *"Did he say 'your room?'* Was the position really hers?" Mr. Severson crossed his arms over his chest, leaned toward her, and then said in a rather somber voice, "Ms. Spencer, before you begin your duties, I must make several points very clear. Some you might find a bit disconcerting, but I am open to comments, questions, and concerns. If, after our conversation, you are willing to move perpetually forward with this position, along with a salary of $125 per week, we are pleased to offer you on-site free room and board. Shall I continue?"

Lydia nodded, wondering why he had used the term *perpetually*. She decided to hear him out first. She could ask questions later.

Mr. Severson nodded back in approval. "The children under your care are very special—very special, indeed. They require an understanding heart, a nonjudgmental attitude, and a willingness to overlook certain…well, certain aspects about their nature." Numbly, Lydia nodded again to show her understanding, if not acceptance. "If you are agreeable to this, then I have been given the authority to offer you the position of first- and second-grade teacher beginning this coming Tuesday."

Lydia felt the warmth of a smile coming up from her heart and playing with the edges of her lips. She looked Mr. Severson right in the eyes and said without hesitation, "I accept."

Mr. Severson clapped his hands, applauding her decision and then exclaimed with outstretched arms, "Excellent! Excellent! Outstanding!" Then in a very grandiose manner, he took his hat from his head and bowed to her. "If you will now excuse me, I have other duties to attend to, Ms. Spencer. I wish you good success and, for the time being, adieu." With that, he turned and left.

Lydia stared after him for a time and then took a much needed breath. She found herself in a tizzy, not knowing what to do first, who to call, or how to celebrate. *Wait! What about a lesson plan?* Mr. Severson had not given her a lesson plan. *Oh dear,* she thought to herself, *and I forgot to ask him about that* perpetual *term.* Well, it was too late now. She would just have to wait and ask him on Tuesday when he was in his principal's office. That gave her pause for thought. She just assumed he was the principal. She giggled under her breath. *Well, of course he was. Who else would he be?*

*   *   *

Although Tuesday was just around the corner, it felt like weeks until the day arrived. She had taken extra care before driving from Push. In a complete state of uncontrolled nerves, she sprayed her brown, bobbed hair with lacquer so many times that it stood stiff. She changed from skirts and light sweaters to her limited supply of dresses and back again several times before choosing what she thought was a smart and professional gray A-line skirt, a double-collared pink blouse, and, of course, her sensible oxfords that had just a hint of height in the heel. Sensible. Everything had to be sensible.

She couldn't take a chance of falling on those entrance steps and she had noticed that the playground was composed of small, round river rock. She would have to have firm footing while monitoring the recesses.

She called her mother several times with the grand news but each time, they had a bad connection. All she could hear was, "Hello, hello?" then a sigh and a hang up. Well, she certainly didn't have time to worry about that now. She would keep trying until she got through. She was just as excited to share the news with her neighbors, but, amazingly, it appeared all eight families had chosen that Labor Day weekend to travel out of town, one last hurrah before the school term began. Over the weekend, she had made a list of questions for Mr. Severson. Among those were: Can you explain the offer of room and board on the premises? Who do I report to? How many other teachers are employed here? What about a lesson plan? What makes these children so special? Truth be told, she only got a few hours of uninterrupted sleep during the entire weekend, waking almost hourly with more questions. But she had to admit, no concerns.

Lydia arrived ninety minutes early. Along with needing the time to compose herself, she wanted to make sure her classroom was in order and that she would have time for the question-and-answer period with Mr. Severson. She pulled into the driveway. Everything looked exactly as it had during her first visit. This time, she noticed an old bus barn standing to the left behind the school. One of the wide open doors was hanging lopsidedly from its upper hinge. There were no buses inside. *Out collecting the children*, she surmised. Above and beyond the barn, she could see a steeple in the distance, rising above some fir trees. It was about a mile away as the crow flies. *There it is*, she thought. Lancaster. Why had she wasted so much precious time fretting all weekend when she could have used it to acclimate to her surroundings and explore the town?

She was quite pleased with herself for being the first one there and the impression that would make on her new principal and the other teachers. She bounded up the stairs, turned the key, and walked inside. She was taken aback when she realized all the other classroom doors were still closed. There were no welcoming banners or calendars of any kind on the walls, just silence. She peeked into two of the classrooms to find them still empty and unprepared. She could hardly believe the incompetency of the rest of the staff. *Don't they care?* In a bit of a huff, she marched down to her own room, walked in and flipped on the light switch. That was better, a place for everything and everything in its place. She walked up the center aisle to her desk. There, sitting on the right-hand corner, was her lesson plan. She mentally checked that question off her list. She sat down at her desk, placed her purse in the bottom drawer, and opened up the lesson plan booklet where she found the first- and second-grade teaching fundamentals for the entire year. She was more than pleased. She looked up at the large, bold-faced clock. How had time gone so fast? It was almost eight. The school bell should be ringing anytime now.

"Ms. Spencer, good morning!" It was that voice again—that baritone, gravelly voice that belonged to Mr. Severson. He was standing just beyond her desk before she noticed that he had even entered the room.

"Good morning," she replied, unable to keep from smiling. "I am so thrilled to be here."

"And we are thrilled to have you, Ms. Spencer. In the next few days, your life will take on a whole new meaning. I know the children will also be thrilled to have you in their lives."

Lydia smiled even broader at the thought of it. "Do they all arrive by bus, and where are the other teachers? Are you the principal? What time are the recesses? Can you point me to the lunchroom?"

Mr. Severson did another of his belly laughs and said, "*Whoa*, a minute, young lady. One question at a time, if you so please."

"I am so sorry. Of course, please forgive me. I think I have allowed myself to go from excited to agitated. That is not the correct persona with which to greet the children for the first time. Please, let me start again. Are you the principal?"

"I am the guardian."

"The guardian?"

"Yes, the guardian."

"The guardian of what?"

"Not what, Ms. Spencer, but *whom*. I am the guardian of the children."

She frowned. "Oh! Well then, who's the principal?"

"There is no principal."

"There is no principal?"

"That is correct, Ms. Spencer. A principal for such a small class is not required."

Her frown deepened. "How big is my class? How about the other classes?"

"You will begin your school year with twelve children, Ms. Spencer. There are no other classes."

"What? Just mine?" That would explain the other empty classrooms.

"Again, that is correct, Ms. Spencer."

"But it is such a large school. How about the other grades? Is this strictly for elementary education or does it include the junior and high school grades."

"It is your class only, Ms. Spencer." This was very discombobulating to Lydia. So discombobulating, in fact, that she forgot what the other questions were.

"It is your first day, Ms. Spencer. Mingled with your excitement and nerves, we can respect that you need to get your bearings. Things will become much clearer as the days go by. I see you have found the lesson plan, and your class room is also the lunchroom. The children always arrive with sack lunches. The recess periods are at ten and two thirty. Lunch is from noon until one o'clock. School is over at four." He paused to see if she was taking this all in. She appeared to be. "The children will be here shortly."

She glanced up at the clock again and was surprised to see the hands still at 7:55 a.m., the same place they had been when their conversation began. She was sure they had conversed for more than five minutes. "I have just one more question about the board and room," she began. But when she looked from the clock to where Mr. Severson had been standing, he was gone. For the first time since her arrival, she felt a bit of trepidation.

"Well, enough of this," she said to herself as she pushed the chair away from her desk and smoothed out nonexistent wrinkles from her skirt. *Let's start with a written introduction.* With that, she turned and picked up the white chalk from its tray and wrote in large, bold letters, "Ms. Spencer." She stepped back and looked at her name in wonder. She had waited so long to do that. Smiling, she turned back toward her classroom. She let out a small gasp. Sitting with hands folded were her twelve students at their small desks. *How in the world did they arrive so quietly?* That was not normal—not for first and second graders. *The poor things.* She could not help but wonder if their specialness was based on abuse. Had that trained them to be silent, speak only when spoken to, and never make noise or out to the woodshed for the strap? Immediately, her heart opened wide, and she fell in love with all twelve of them at the same time.

By first recess, she knew each of them by name. She was right— they were sponges, eager and wide-eyed, raising their hands to be called on before asking questions and saying her name with awe in their little voices. Lydia was too focused on them to even think back to any trepidation she may have had. These were her special students, and they needed her. She would heap into their brains and hearts all the knowledge and love she had within her.

First recess was nothing if not delightful. She laughed with them as she pushed them on the swings higher and higher into the clear autumn sky. She stood at the bottom of the slide to catch them if they needed catching. They were just as she had imagined—laughing and poking, running and jabbing, but all in good sport. They were filled with so much energy yet so well-behaved. How blessed she felt. This had to be the most perfect group of students she would ever tutor, and she planned to cherish every moment before they moved on.

Somehow, the days turned into weeks and the weeks into months. Lydia continued to be enamored with her students, and her educational skills blossomed as each new week went by. She could not have been more content nor fulfilled. Their arrival had become a game to her. Each morning at exactly eight, she would turn to the blackboard and write "Good morning, my very special students" with two exclamation points, knowing that when she turned back toward the room, they would all be there with hands folded, waiting expectantly at their desks. It only took one time for her to realize that at the end of each school day, they would not leave until she once again faced the blackboard and wrote, "Good day, my loves." Each time she turned back, they were gone. Someone else might have found this odd, but Lydia found it to be endearing. She gave it no further thought. They were, after all, special.

The round-trips from Push had become cumbersome. It broke her heart each time she pulled away for what had become the long trip home. Inner peace came only when she was near her children. She arrived each morning before dawn and left after dusk. With winter coming on, the roads were beginning to ice up. She even saw a car flip over into the ditch. The car behind her stopped to assist so she continued on her way. The idea of room and board was becoming increasingly attractive.

Mr. Severson had a ritual. He showed up every Friday after the children left for the day. He knew she was content because she had stopped asking questions. It did not matter one iota that she had the whole school building to herself. She didn't care about being the only teacher. Her entire existence became wrapped up in her students. They were all she cared about. Her Friday meetings with Mr. Severson consisted of discussing the students' progress and the matter of supplies. Mr. Severson couldn't have been more pleased. At their last meeting, Mr. Severson once again broached the topic of room and board. "Our offer still stands, Ms. Spencer."

As fate would have it, the decision was made for her. She saw the plume of black smoke the moment Push came into sight. Her heart sank. Instinctively, she knew. She gasped, and her heart began racing at the thought of Panda being trapped in the trailer and burned alive. She pulled into the trailer park just behind the Patterson fire trucks. But it was too late. Nothing was left but a pile of smoldering ashes. Slowly, she opened the car door and sank to her knees the minute her feet hit the ground. She covered her eyes and began sobbing. *Panda, Panda! My poor little Panda.* She felt the soft touch of fur against her body before she heard the meow.

"Oh, Panda, you're alive!" She scooped him into her arms and hugged him so tightly that he actually grunted. She watched as the firemen began sifting through the rubble and hosing down any smoldering embers. They were so focused on making sure the fire was contained, they didn't even notice her. The neighbors were all in a tizzy, hugging their own pets close to their chests and shaking their heads at the tragedy of it all. There was nothing left for Lydia to do. Not today, if ever. Any reports or paperwork that needed to be taken care of, she would tend to another day. She got back into her car, placed Panda on the seat beside her, and drove away.

She had to wait an entire week before Friday rolled around again so she could talk with Mr. Severson. She had come to terms with her loss in less than a moment. Now that it was gone, she realized she had actually hated that cramped little trailer. All her belongings were replaceable. For whatever reason, the neighbors stopped being friendly just about the time she had taken on her teaching position. At times, she felt like they were actually avoiding her. She was glad to be done with the place.

Mr. Severson appeared promptly at four. He had a look of satisfaction on his face. He bent, ever so slightly, over her desk and whispered, "I am so sorry for your loss." *He knew!* Well, of course. It was probably in the local paper that she never read. "Shall we finalize the offer?" He smiled sweetly.

This time, Lydia didn't hesitate. "I do believe I have no choice than to take you up on your generous offer, Mr. Severson." With that, her future was firmly cemented into place. "Where will my quarters be?"

Mr. Severson swept his hand toward the door, and she followed him up a back staircase. The entire second floor had been remodeled into an apartment. It was much too large for her needs, but in time, Lydia somehow utilized all the available space. Except for the bathroom, there were wood-burning fireplaces in each of the other four rooms, which were her bedroom, a parlor, an office, and a combination kitchen and dining area. Lydia was amazed at Mr. Severson's kindness and efficiency. Each afternoon when she turned off the lights in her classroom and climbed the seventeen stairs to her suite, fresh wood had been stacked at each location and the fires were always burning brightly. All she had to do was stoke them during the evening. Upon waking in the morning, there were enough embers left to relight the wood so she was never cold. *And the food!* She wasn't sure how Mr. Severson knew her likes and dislikes (no beets, no brussel sprouts, and definitely no cottage cheese!), but her pantry and icebox were consistently filled with only the items she liked. It slipped Lydia's mind to resolve any insurance issues regarding the trailer fire.

Christmas was right around the corner, and what fun the children had tromping through the snow at the back of the property finding the right evergreen. They all took turns chopping it down with an old axe Lydia found in the bus barn. Then the fun really started with decorating, tree-trimming, making presents for each other, and singing Christmas carols. They even baked cookies in the old cafeteria oven. Sometimes Lydia thought she would burst from happiness. Not only were these her students, they were her longed-for family. She had not thought about a husband and children of her own since her position began. In fact, that concept felt rather foreign to her now.

She finally found time to explore Lancaster. It was a four-street town with nothing much more than a tavern, a mercantile, a small church, a town hall, and a combination savings and loan with a post office. She did not, however, have to frequent the post office. If ever there was mail, which was nothing more than a few periodicals and an occasional advertisement, she would find it neatly placed on the parlor table. With time, she knew that any outgoing mail she placed on that table would be gone when she returned from class each afternoon.

She would never forget the date: January 14th. It was the afternoon that Mr. Severson towered above her desk with a yellow envelope in his hands. There was doom in those lifeless eyes, dulling the rest of his countenance as he handed her the envelope. She fainted. When she awoke, she was lying across the couch in her parlor with the envelope still clutched in her hand. Mr. Severson sat stiffly across from her in the Queen Anne parlor chair.

"I am so sorry, Ms. Spencer."

Her mom and pops were dead. It was a car accident. She had no details. That was all the telegram stated. Just like that, gone. She later learned that Pops evidently ran a red light in town, and a delivery truck sideswiped them with such force that the car flipped over twice before landing upside down. Drunk, she was sure of it. She wanted to curse him but in respect for the dead, she put that thought out of her mind and said a silent prayer for her mother instead. There was no funeral. Lydia opted for cremation and placed the urns filled with their ashes into the deep, dark hole at the plot pops had purchased when he first married. Even though he was stingy with his life, he had made it a point to see that they were taken care of in death.

The telephone never rang in the school house but a week after the burial, Lydia had to excuse herself from class, race down the hallway, and grab the receiver from its cradle on the wall before the caller could hang up. "Hello?"

"Ms. Spencer?"

"Speaking."

"This is Mr. Jackson, your parents' attorney."

"Attorney?"

"Yes, Ms. Spencer. I need to talk with you about their will."

"Their will?"

"Yes, Ms. Spencer. I would love to meet with you but as events turn out, I will be on the East Coast for the next three weeks. I would be more than willing to put the check in the mail. Also, you will need to sign several documents that I will include in that mailing. Please have them notarized before you return them. Will that work for you?"

Mr. Severson came up behind her and whispered coarsely in her ear, "I know a notary."

"Yes, yes, that would be fine."

Lydia hung up the receiver wide-eyed. She did not know her folks had an attorney, let alone a will. Within 24 hours, Lydia went from being just a daughter to a daughter with a $40,000 inheritance. How her mother had managed to save up that much money, she would never know. She was in shock for several days until it finally sunk in. She had means. Not knowing what to do with those means at that particular time, she immediately took it to the savings and loan in Lancaster and deposited it within her already healthy savings account fund from her paychecks. It had not taken long to accumulate just under $5,000 in pay, and it was all there. She had no needs that required money. She had room and board. If she ever needed her car, it was always oiled, gassed, and ready to drive. She really had no interest in new clothes. The ones she had were more than suitable. Her life was now fully devoted to her students and to her students only.

As circumstances would have it, she happened to be at recess when she noticed an old Ford pickup parked with the engine idling at the top of the hill. Two old geezers were looking down and watching her. Their window was open. What she heard shocked her beyond belief. She ended recess fifteen minutes early, stationed the children at their desks, and ordered them to color a picture she handed out. They were all stunned. They had never seen Ms. Spencer in such a state. This was the first time she had ever ordered them to do anything. Quietly, they obeyed, raising their eyebrows at each other as she stomped out of the room.

"Mr. Severson! Mr. Severson!" She raced down the hallway, into the cafeteria, and up and down the stairs calling his name over and over again. He had to be here someplace, he always was, even if he didn't make himself known. She rounded a corner, and had he not glided out of the way, she would have smacked right into him. "Mr. Severson!" she practically screeched at him. "What in the world is going on?" Mr. Severson watched her with his deep, penetrating eyes but said nothing. She tapped her foot impatiently. "When were you going to tell me? What is to become of me? Of the children?" She saw her whole life crashing down before her eyes.

"What is it, Ms. Spencer?"

Lydia looked at him in disbelief. *How could he not know?* She crossed her arms over her chest and leaning toward him with wild eyes glaring into his vacant ones, hissed "How long have you known the school was up for sale?"

Mr. Severson raised his eyebrows but was undaunted. He bent down and leaned into Lydia's space. "What makes you think that, Ms. Spencer?"

"I heard two old men talking. They said that since no buyer had been found during the past ten years, it was going to go on the auction block next month."

It was a standoff. Neither moved an inch as they glared at each other. Mr. Severson absolutely loathed confrontation and bristled at Ms. Spencer usurping his authority and control over things. Things had always been done his way and would continue to be done his way with or without Ms. Spencer. Lydia was feeling uncomfortable being that close to those dead eyes staring into hers. *Didn't he understand that this was not just her life they were talking about, but her entire existence?* Although she had begun shaking, she held her ground.

"So how long have you known, Mr. Severson?" she spat out more harshly than she had intended.

"Forever."

"What is *that* supposed to mean?"

Mr. Severson straightened back up, smiled a crooked smile, and reached out to put his hand on her shoulder. Lydia jerked away. It was the first time he tried to touch her. "That means, Ms. Spencer, that I understand the situation and it is well under control."

"I see, and you didn't think it was important enough to tell me?"

"So you could go into this semicatatonic state—as you obviously have—and lose all sense of propriety? I have it under control, Ms. Spencer."

"And how is that, Mr. Severson?"

"Who better to own this property than you, Ms. Spencer?"

"What?"

"You purchase it." The silence was palatable. Lydia thought he was being ridiculous and crazy all at the same time. Before she could respond, he continued, "You have the financial resources now. A deed in your name would prevent any further interference from the outside world. Not only would the children be safer, you would own the entire property to do with as you see fit. You could repair, remodel, and turn the cafeteria into the gymnasium you have talked about for so long so the children have a warm, dry place for recess in the winter months." He watched her.

Her mind was spinning. *What a grand idea!* Her heart began to beat faster. Yes, of course. Why hadn't she thought of it herself? It made all the sense in the world. She would put a fence around the entire perimeter, a high eight-foot fence so no intruders could disrupt the safety and peace of her children. She shuddered when she remembered the kid from town who had driven into the property. He sat in his souped-up blue Chevy and stared at her for the longest time during recess. When she walked over to confront him, he fishtailed back up to the road before she could say a word. Yes. Safety. Privacy. No intruders. Yes, this was a perfect idea.

Lydia smiled. "How do I go about doing this?"

Mr. Severson returned her smile. "Send a certified letter to Lancaster City Council and make an offer they cannot refuse."

Her students had become her family and now the old school would become her home. She could barely instruct the students during the rest of the week. The letter was in the mail. The meeting was the next Wednesday. She wanted to attend but Mr. Severson talked her out of it, stating they would need some time to mull it over first.

*   *   *

It was a small, informal setting. Two large, paned windows faced east, allowing the midmorning sun to stream in and warm the room. A solid oak conference table took up most of the space. By the time the four councilmen pushed their chairs into place, there was barely room to maneuver. Three chairs were stacked against the back wall for the use of citizens who were allowed to listen to proceedings at will. It was in this room that motions were made on all matters, large and small, seconded and approved or tabled for more research and discussion. Generally, they were necessary but petty matters. Should they finally approve a stop sign at the intersection of Main and First streets? Should Mrs. Gerber be allowed to have more than six chickens on her municipal property?

"Now for the main topic of discussion," said Joe Baker, the middle-aged, balding chairman, as he looked over his spectacles at the other councilmen, "the old school building and property."

A low moan went around the table. Not again. This topic had been broached and tabled for well over ten years. During that time, a young hippie couple had the eye-rolling idea of turning the building into a hemp clothing store and gift shop and wanted to hold stained-glass-window-making classes. They didn't have the resources to make a down payment but just assumed that because the building sat vacant for so many years, the council would jump all over a meager monthly payment. Mike Johnson, the only contractor in the area, wanted to raze the whole thing and develop the acreage into high-rise apartments and condos. Trouble was, there wasn't enough industry nor potential tenants to support that idea. This was a farming community after all. Mildred Banks and her group of civic-minded ladies had been fighting for years to have the old school designated as an historical site. Throughout the years, all the pros-and-cons discussions stalemated. This time was different. The chairman had received a letter from some lady who wanted to buy it straight out. It was a tempting thought to be done with it once and for all even though he didn't understand why and for what purpose she wanted it. Kids hadn't attended there for over a decade, not since the fancy, modern school was built on the other side of town.

"I thought we were going to auction it off next month," Jess Woelk said grumpily. He had fishing gear packed and ready to go in the back of his truck, and the last thing he wanted to do was rehash the old school.

"Yes, we were. But I have a letter here I would like to read you. It may preempt the necessity of an auction."

"Okay, read it."

"It's pretty short and sweet," the chairman replied. He cleared his throat and began reading.

> *To Whom It May Concern:*
> *Please be advised that it is my intent to purchase the Lancaster District 4 public school house and all adjoining property. I have the financial means to pay cash in the sum of $40,000 as long as the terms are agreed upon and accepted within the next thirty days. Please reply via certified mail.*
>
> *Sincerely,*
> *Lydia Spencer*
> *Schoolmarm*
> *Lancaster School District 4*

"So what do you think?" Joe said to no one in particular.

"Who in the world is Lydia Spencer?" Jess asked.

The Chairman shrugged. "Never heard of her. I had Leona delve into the school records, and she couldn't find hide nor hair of her ever being employed by the district."

"Who the hell cares?" came from Pete Schierman. "For $40,000, I say we call off the auction and give her the deed. Scuttlebutt around town is no one is interested in buying. We'd be lucky to get a tenth of that at auction."

There was silence as each councilman thought it over. Finally, Jess said, "I make a motion that we sell that old albatross *as is* to this Ms. Spencer for $40,000."

"Don't you think that is a little premature?" asked Jake Arvidson. "We don't know anything about this woman, let alone what she plans to do with the property. Sure, the profits could be put to good use, but the building is pretty derelict as it stands. What if she buys it and then ignores it completely? We would eventually have an even bigger eyesore for the folks driving by as they come into town. You think we have complaints now!"

"What did the letter say? Did it mention improvements? Did she imply why she wanted the property and what she plans to use it for?" asked Jess who had been mentally fishing on Trout Lake and hadn't really listened to the reading.

"Nope," responded Joe. "Just that she wants it and the offer has to be accepted in thirty days."

"Well, she signed it as *schoolmarm*. Wouldn't that indicate to you that she has plans to maintain it as a school," Jess interjected.

Joe frowned at Jess over his spectacles. "For whom, pray tell?"

Jess shrugged. "Maybe she is going to open up some kind of beauty school or technical school or who the heck knows school. Has she applied for a permit?"

With that, Joe lost a little patience. "Hey, Jess! Join the group here, will ya? There will be plenty of daylight left for fishing. Why, pray tell, would she apply for a permit before she owned the property?" Joe shook his head and continued, "Does anyone else have something productive to add?" Jess snorted but remained silent.

"Maybe she is planning to tear it down and build a brand-new building," Pete ventured hopefully.

"That would solve a lot of woes," Jake nodded. "But we don't know that."

"Why do we need to know? I say, take the money and run," Pete said firmly as he slapped one hand on the table.

Suddenly, the atmosphere in the room changed. As the years went by, their immediate and decisive action to approve would be rehashed over and over but no one was ever able to explain it.

As if in a stupor, Jess made a motion to sell, Jake seconded, and Joe slammed his gavel on the table at the same time he said, "Approved!"

The entire transaction was done through certified mail with the documents all signed and notarized. The entire process took less than ten days. No one ever met Ms. Spencer. The day the bill of sale arrived, a joyful Ms. Spencer was in her parlor, focused intently on folding the document so it would fit into an ornate, wooden frame she found in the attic. It would hang over the parlor fireplace, drawing her attention every time she entered the room and reminding her of her good fortune. She could not stop smiling. She heard a clink behind her and realized Mr. Severson was standing in her kitchen with two crystal goblets in hand.

"I believe a toast is in order, Ms. Spencer."

Lydia starred at him. "Why, Mr. Severson, I do not imbibe."

He threw his head back and bellowed. "A little sherry never hurt anyone, Ms. Spencer. It is actually good for the soul." He bowed slightly as he reached out and handed her the glass.

Lydia smiled nervously. This did call for a celebration after all. "Well, just a sip," she gave in reluctantly as she raised the goblet to her lips.

"Wait!" Mr. Severson startled her. "The toast first!" She blushed. She knew so little of the ways of the world. "To you, Ms. Spencer.

Without you, none of this could have happened. May you rest in peace."

Lydia thought that a rather odd toast but she raised her glass nonetheless. For the first time, she genuinely smiled at him. The burning liquid made her eyes water, and she sputtered. The taste was not unpleasant. She sank back into the cushions, enjoying the calming effect it was having on her. Without a second thought, she held out her goblet for a second pour. Thereafter, at the end of each teaching day, she would find an uncorked bottle of sherry waiting for her on the parlor table. She approved.

It was such a lovely life. Even though there was no variation from day to day, she thrived on the clockwork precision of each moment. Time had lost all meaning. The bold-faced round clock on her classroom wall was either at exactly eight or four o'clock. She knew the routine and her children so well that she no longer depended on a schedule. She wasn't even sure how many months had slipped by or was it years? Lydia was still young, not quite thirty. There was no good reason she should be losing her mental capacities, and yet, if one thing haunted her, it was the urgent feeling that there was something vitally important she was supposed to tend to. Something that required her attention; something about a fence. But as soon as the thought began to form, it was gone again. It was very satisfying to shrug it off and turn back to her comfortable routine.

* * *

Late one spring, Jake and Pete were on their way to Trout Lake for a promising day of fishing.

Pete detoured onto the road that went past the old school. "I want to show you something," he said to Jake. There was a slight breeze blowing as he pulled to the side of the road at the top of the hill and shut off the engine. "Watch."

Jake looked down at the old school and watched. He saw nothing out of the ordinary. He shook his head at the dilapidated building half hidden in the overgrown weeds. He had tried to warn the other councilmen years ago that this would happen. "What?" he snapped at Pete, impatient to get to the lake.

"Watch that middle swing."

Jake watched. It was gliding back and forth slightly in the breeze. After staring for a few seconds, he threw up his hand and looked at Pete. "Yeah – so?"

"Just watch."

Jake rolled his eyes and continued watching. He watched while the swing went up and down higher and higher. He frowned. The breeze wasn't that strong. He glanced over at Pete.

"See!" Pete practically yelled at him. "You can't tell me that isn't odd. I've never seen a swing act like that. It's like there is weight on it, like someone is sitting on it, or,"—he hesitated—"like someone is pushing it." They both looked at each other and got goose bumps at the same time. "I've pulled over and watched it a hundred times. It's not always the middle swing. Sometimes it's all of them."

As if on cue, the swing farthest from them began its upward and downward motion.

"That's not odd," Pete said a little shaken, "That's downright spooky. Let's get out of here."

*   *   *

The children disappeared for the day. Lydia caught her breath. It was the first time she referred to them as disappearing rather than leaving. But when she thought about it, that is basically what they had been doing all this time, appearing and disappearing. She tried to think that through but, once again, the thought drifted into the back of her mind and vaporized. She decided to get some fresh air. It was an amazingly warm day, and she felt a surge of spring fever coming on. She had wandered most of the property with her children, exploring the grounds, making a tally of the number of different birds they spotted, and cataloging the different types of flowers and plants. She realized her favorite time was when she was outside with them.

Every so often, she would pass by what remained of a tree trunk from the times they chopped down their Christmas trees. She was surprised at the number of them. She ventured behind the bus barn, a place not yet explored due to the overgrown weeds. She was just ready to turn back when she stubbed her toe on something hard hidden in the underbrush. She had hit the edge of what appeared to be a slab of concrete. She knelt down and began pulling the weeds and tall grasses that had grown up over it.

When she came to, she wondered why she was dizzy and disoriented. It took her a moment to get her bearings and remember where she was and what she had seen. She bit her bottom lip as she pulled herself into a sitting position on the ground. It took all the strength she had to look back down at the slab.

> Lydia Suzanne Spencer
> December 20, 1937 – September 3, 1964
> RIP

She sensed the presence of Mr. Severson before she actually felt his hand on her shoulder. He said nothing. There was nothing to be said. Finally, Lydia broke the silence. "Nothing is making sense," she stated flatly. "Nothing fits."

Mr. Severson gently squeezed her shoulder, as her mind flashed back to the major events in her life. The car she had watched flip into the icy ditch—that had been her. Her neighbors in Push—they weren't avoiding her, they couldn't see her. The trailer fire. It made sense now why no one tried to finalize insurance matters, she was already dead. How excited she had been to share the good news about her teaching position with her mother. No wonder she only said, "Hello, hello?" She couldn't hear her. But the timing of these matters was all off.

As if reading her mind, Mr. Severson stated matter-of-factly, "There is no time in death."

She suddenly remembered the urgent task she was supposed to take care of: remodeling the school, putting up an eight-foot-high safety fence, and getting the old girl back to her original splendor with the money she had acquired over the years. She thought back to the original bill of sale, framed and hanging over her parlor fireplace. It was real. It had happened. She could get up right this minute, march into that parlor, and take if off the wall to touch it and read those wonderful words that gave her ownership. It was too much to take in.

"The children still need you, Ms. Spencer," Mr. Severson said kindly, hoping to ease her growing agitation.

It worked. She took a deep breath—at least it felt like a real breath—and let some of the tension flow out of her body. She thought about all the money she so faithfully deposited in her savings account each and every month alongside the remainder of her inheritance. "What about the money? Where is all the money?" she almost whimpered.

"All we needed was ownership, Ms. Spencer, and that we got. Many of our experiences, whether in life or death, are just a figment of our imagination. Have you even noticed the premises, Ms. Spencer? More plaster has fallen; there is a continuous overgrowth of weeds that has almost drowned the entire property." Lydia stopped and thought, realizing that she had not. "The children don't notice either. Their lives are centered around you, Ms. Spencer, and your life around them. That is all that matters. That is what will go on perpetually."

Lydia tried to take this all in. The timing still eluded her. How had she been able to make deposits into a nonexistent checking account? She tried in vain to put it all in a sensible timeline but, once again and for the final time, the thought slipped into the back of her mind and faded away forever. She didn't know when it happened but she realized her hand was resting on Mr. Severson's leg. She raised her head and looked into those once dead eyes that now were moist and shining.

"Oh, my!" was all she could muster.

Bradley

It was a strange sensation. The white, tiled wall he had been star-ing at as the belt tightened around his neck vaporized into a 3D illusion. His depth perception pierced through the cold reality of those porcelain squares and opened up a whole new dimension of sight. He could not identify the shiver that went through him but he knew for certain something was different.

He found himself gazing into an aura of breathtaking colors. He knew the colors of the rainbow but never colors like this. Logically, he should have been able to identify each one, call to mind the color chart, and give each its proper name. But these shimmering hues were not on any color chart he had ever seen. As the edges of the haze began to drift away, he was able to make out lush green grass with a luminous pathway winding through it. Someone was walking up the pathway but was too far away for him to identify.

He felt a presence near his right shoulder and looked up. A most wondrous being was smiling down at him. Then he remembered. He had seen this amazing sentinel just before his gaze had gone beyond those bathroom tiles. "Oh!" he said out loud, now understanding. "You're my guardian angel."

The angel nodded, and with a slight bow, he said, "It has been my pleasure to serve you these past 16 years. Welcome to your new home."

75

Now he really understood. He wanted to think about and analyze this revelation but he was having trouble remembering. His mind would not let him play backward, only forward. The figure on the path was coming more clearly into view. The closer he approached, the more stunned Bradley became. It was Jesus. At that, his mind did a double take. *How in the world could he know that? He'd never before seen Jesus.* But it was Jesus, all right. He just knew. Bradley was greeted with the most warm, welcoming smile. Jesus' arms were outstretched, inviting him into the safe haven of His embrace. Bradley found himself enveloped before he realized he had moved toward Him.

"Hello, Bradley. I have been waiting for this moment for a very long time."

"Jesus." It was all Bradley could say. It was not a question. It was not a statement. It was a culmination of sound truth. Jesus, the Great I Am.

"Come, sit and talk with me for a while," Jesus said as he led him toward a large rock by a shimmering stream.

Bradley was becoming more aware of his surroundings, which seemed surreal in comparison to the solid presence of Jesus by his side. As he sat down beside Jesus, he tried to find the right words with which to address his Savior. He was truly dumbfounded. No words seemed appropriate. Besides, he really didn't want to speak. He just wanted to bask in this all-encompassing love and perfection. He was afraid that if he closed his eyes, it would all go away, taking him with it. Where it would take him, he didn't know. He only knew he would no longer be able to endure without Him. He hesitated. *How do you address Jesus? Sir? Master? O Holy One?* He looked up at Jesus who was smiling fully into Bradley's eyes, looking almost amused.

"You can call me *friend*."

Friend, really? That seemed too much to hope for. Bradley didn't know if he deserved that. He glanced up at Jesus again. The welcoming smile was still on His face. *Wow! He really means it. I can call him friend.*

Bradley smiled and suddenly felt like he had been in Jesus' presence his whole life. "Well, my *friend*," he started without hesitation, "I don't know what to say. I'm so overwhelmed to be here, to be with you. I am not sure how I even got here." Before the last word was out of his mouth, Jesus gave him an instantaneous flashback. "Oh no! No, no, no. What did I do?" Bradley cried out. "What was I thinking? Oh, my mother, my family! Will they ever forgive me? Can You ever forgive me?"

Just as instantaneously, Jesus wiped the picture from Bradley's mind but not the memory of it.

"Bradley, I did forgive you. I forgave you before you were even born."

"How old were you when you realized I was your Savior and that I died just for you, just for your sins?"

Bradley didn't have to think long about that question because Jesus gave him another earthly remembrance. "I was eight," Bradley replied.

"And when did you stop believing in me?" Jesus continued.

Bradley sat stunned. Like a quick succession of Morse code dots and dashes, Jesus flashed moments of reality into Bradley's mind; some of which made him cringe and some he would just as soon not remember. But with each flash, it became clearer to Bradley. There was no doubt. He jumped up from the rock he was sitting on and almost danced with joy. "Oh, dear friend! I never did stop believing in you!"

Jesus continued smiling. These were some of His favorite times—the times when it all became clear to His creation.

"I just…I just…I…" Bradley stammered.

"Just got bombarded by darts from the evil one and didn't know how to counter them due to your lack of knowledge," Jesus finished for him.[1]

---

[1]   My people are destroyed from their lack of knowledge. Hosea 4:6 (NIV)

Bradley hung his head…not in shame, but in humbleness. "Oh, friend Jesus, thank you. Thank you for sticking with me during the traumas of my life."

"My pleasure."

"And please forgive me for not doing more for you while I was on earth. In fact, I feel like I did nothing at all."

"Oh, but you did, Bradley. You did the main and only thing truly required of you—you believed in me."[2]

Could it be that simple? Bradley thought.

"There were things in your life that, at the appointed time, will be burned up like chaff to be remembered no more. The good things you did in your life will be rewarded."

But, thought Bradley, *I can't remember any good things I did. Not really.*

Again, Jesus flashed events into his mind, causing Bradley's smile to return. He was amazed at how precious his life had been. He was shown moments of compassion, times of giving, and instances of love and loyalty to friends. He sat with his hand on Jesus' knee, bursting with gratitude that his life on earth had truly mattered. Jesus continued to weave memories into a grand eternal tapestry, making it very apparent to Bradley that he had been an integral part of this plan long before time began. Bradley rested his head on Jesus' shoulder and let out a long, cleansing sigh.

"Bradley, in time, you will find that I am more than enough."

Bradley continued to smile. He already was.

*   *   *

---

[2]   "Then they asked him what must we do to do the works God requires?" Jesus answered, "The work of God is this: to believe in the one he has sent." John 6:28-29 (NIV)

Further on in a realm that Bradley could not see, Lucifer had once again gained entrance into the courts of heaven[3] to come before God Almighty with a list of accusations against numerous of His earthly creatures.[4] He flung the list open in a show of one-upmanship, the length of the cross-folds, skirting out several yards behind him. He relished his appointed times before God's throne when he could throw the sins of one of his precious creation right in his Almighty face. The part he despised, however, was being denied direct contact with this alleged Supreme God. There was a veil of holiness between him and the Creator. If he squinted, he could just barely make out His image, sitting there all high and mighty on His throne. Throughout the centuries, he tried in vain several times to break through that veil but each time, he was hurled out of the throne room by the sentry angels posted at intervals along its circumference. He had finally given up. It didn't matter. His intent, his only reason for existing was to claim that throne for himself before all was said and done.

"Well, *your majesty*, I am humbled to be in your presence once again," he mocked. "I will try not to take up too much of your precious time, but as you can see, the list is quite long this time." His whole countenance writhed in glee. There was no response from the throne. "Yes. Well then, let me begin." Laboriously, Lucifer went through the list: the murderers in Minnesota, the incest in California, the sex traders in India, and the continuing sins that circled the globe. He paused when he got to the cursers worldwide. "Let me save us both precious time. Rather than read this portion, I will just say, *oh mighty*

---

[3]   "One day the angels came to present themselves before the Lord, and Satan also came with them." Job 1:6 (NIV)

[4]   Then I heard a loud voice in heaven say: "Now have come the salvation and the power and the kingdom of our God, and the authority of his Christ. For the accuser of our brothers, who accuses them before our God day and night, has been hurled down." Revelation 12:10 (NIV)

one, more of your creation is taking your name in vain than praising it." He snorted.

He waited. More silence. God really had a way of grating on his nerves.

"Continuing on then, *your holiness*." A third of the way through the list, he spat out the name "Bradley Collins."

"Look behind you," came the thundering voice from the throne.

Lucifer had to brace himself against the reverberation. He reached out to steady himself, grabbing at one of the sentries. All he touched was his robe, which was immediately wrenched out of his grasp. *How quaint*, he sneered. *Evil can never touch good in the heavenly realm of the King's court.* He turned and gazed down at the scene by a stream of water. Someone was sitting and conversing intimately with Jesus. Just to have to think the name *Jesus* brought a guttural growl from deep within his being; to look upon him was sheer torture. "Who is that?" he asked one of the sentries.

"Look closer," was the only response.

With penetrating, beady little eyes, he bent down and peered more closely. He then shot back up with a start. It was Bradley Collins. He wasn't supposed to be here. Lucifer was furious, absolutely livid. He tried to maintain his composure before these annoying sentries whose faces always lit up like the sun when they experienced complete joy. "You haven't seen the last of me!" he spat at them.

But they had already fallen on their faces before God, praising Him for His mighty works. In one forceful blast of wind, he was hurled out of God's presence. Lucifer raged and spewed fire all the way back to his kingdom headquarters. He screeched out the name Apollyon,[5] his highest commander of Legions.

A moment did not elapse before Apollyon was bowing in his presence. "Yes, my liege, I am forever at your service."[5]

---

[5] "They had a king over them, the angel of the Abyss, whose name in Hebrew is Abaddon, and in Greek, Apollyon." Revelation 9:11 (NIV)

"Take a look at this!" Lucifer raged at him while flashing a picture of Jesus and Bradley laughing and slapping hands at some maddening goodness that must have happened on earth. Lucifer slithered up to within inches of Apollyon's face. "You had better fix this!"

Apollyon rose up to his full eight-foot frame. Bowing once again, he disappeared. Instantaneously, he appeared in a dim, dank little room inhabited by a dozen or so lesser demons who all seemed on edge and were making it a point to stay a safe distance—as if there was such a thing—from Abigor.

Abigor, the commander and battalion leader for Legion 6626 had been pacing for over twenty-four earthly hours, waiting and dreading. He turned midpace and bumped squarely into the imposing figure of Apollyon who had fire in his eyes and a rancid stench coming out of his nostrils. Abigor immediately fell to his knees. Trying unsuccessfully to keep the quiver out of his voice, he whispered, "My liege."

Apollyon began turning over tables and slamming frog-faced demons against the wall. "What are the rules?" he bellowed. "How many eons do we have to go over them? If you cannot properly do your job, I know hordes of others who can." His features became even more distorted with rage.

"Yes, my liege. The rules must be obeyed."

"Then why weren't they?" he howled in a high-pitched wail as he kicked one of the cowering demons with such force that it went hurling through the air, breaking a window and screeching in terror out into the unknown. "Gather your troops." Without hesitation, the members of Legion 6626 who were present scurried to find a place to sit at the feet of their leader. "Let us go over this one more time," Apollyon rumbled in short, staccato words.

Backing away from his still seething superior, Abigor began to recite, "We are to steal all hope. We are to kill all ambition. We are to destroy all faith."

"*Hmmm.* Three such simple, little tasks," Apollyon mused. "How could you possibly fail?" They both knew to whom he was referring—Bradley Collins. "Let me ask you this," Apollyon said, feigning ignorance. "How often are you to do these three little tasks?"

"As often as required, my liege," replied Abigor.

"Yes, yes, that is quite true." He began walking around the room, looking directly into the eyes of all the demons. Cringing, they all tried to shrink to a smaller size and out of his piercing gaze. "And, if I may, how far do you go in carrying out these teeny, tiny, minute tasks?"

Abigor swallowed hard. "Up to, but not including, death."

With that, Apollyon spew out more venom than the little room could hold. The temperature climbed 90 degrees. Yellow smoke filled every nook and cranny, and the entire Legion scattered into corners with great trembling. His foul presence permeated the air.

"Because of your incompetence, we have lost another one!" he roared. He began pounding his clawed fist on the table. "Up to, up to, up to! Get it? Not past, UP TO! You lead *up to* despair, not past it. You lead *up to* depression, not past it. You lead *up to* failure, not past it! You back away if it becomes obvious that someone is on the point of breaking. Do you understand? For the very final time, do you understand? Your only task on earth is to make their lives miserable. Once they are gone, you can't very well do that now, can you?" Trying to break away from the fire in Apollyn's gaze, all Abigor could do was shake his head. "So now that we've lost him, do I have to tell you whose *comforting arms* he is in?" he sneered.

"Jesus?"

His eight-foot stature loomed over the room as he hissed, "Who said that? Which of you slimy, little, no-good dungs had the audacity to say that name in my presence?" The silence was deafening. Everyone knew that Lucifer's right hand man could and would wait out that silence until the culprit showed himself. Finally, one puny paw was raised ever so slightly. Apollyon glared and pointed a bent and crooked talon at him. *Poof!* He was gone in a whiff of vapor. Then Apollyon turned himself into a sickening, smelly viper and curled his way around each member of Legion 6626. "Don't ever, *ever* say that name in my presence." Then, as if nothing had happened, he materialized back into his eight-foot being and addressed Abigor once again. "Where is the rest of your Legion?"

"They are on whisper detail."

"Good, good. And who is their main target?"

"The mother."

"Ah, very good!" He smiled.

"Which whisperers have you commissioned?"

"The spirits of Depression and Guilt."

"Very good. Don't you think it would be wise to also send the spirits of Unforgiveness and Illness?"

"Yes, yes, of course." Abigor snapped his fingers, and the two spirits left the room.

"Lucifer is not happy. He is ready to send your entire Legion to the lowest bowels of the earth." All the demons glanced at each other in total dismay. They all knew what that meant—an eternity of polishing talons, shining scales, and being mocked and spat upon by the higher echelon of Lucifer's kingdom. "Now we wouldn't want that, would we?" Apollyon ridiculed. All the demons shook their heads. "Then get it right!" he snarled as his fist came down on the last remaining table. Then he disappeared.

The demons wished it was over but they knew the fury of Abigor was yet to be reckoned with. They were a bit taken back with Abigor's controlled rage. Feigning calmness, he pointed at three of them and ordered them to stay incognito and hidden from view while standing guard over the whisperers. They were to make sure that the whispers going into the mother's subconscious ear were done forcefully and convincingly, and if not, to report back to him immediately.

"But we have to contend with the Guardians," one demon whined.

Abigor whirled around and grabbed him by his scrawny, little throat. "Is this job too hard for you? Would you like me to replace you with someone who can handle it?"

"No, no, it's not too hard. I can do this. It's just…"

"What?" Abigor tightened his grip around his throat.

"It's just that every time one of the whisperers performs his task, a Guardian is whispering in the other ear and,"—he gulped, squirming for air—"and…well, she is starting to listen to the Guardians instead of us."

Abigor slammed the demon onto the floor. "You are just now telling me this? Do you have any idea what it means to report back to me? Don't you understand that greater powers need to be called in? What is wrong with all of you inept, no-good curs?"

"Well, sir, with all due respect, every time you call in higher powers, the Guardians send in higher powers of their own." Apollyon rolled his blood-stained eyes. He was working with morons. "Who's going to win, boss?"

Apollyon bent low and hissed at the demon, "Well, that is entirely her choice now, isn't it?"

*   *   *

Jesus and Bradley had been sitting together in close companionship for quite a long time. With no earthly time in heaven, Bradley didn't know if it had been hours, days, or just seconds.[6] He only knew he never wanted it to end. A sudden gush of putrid decay swept over them.

---

[6]   "But do not forget this one thing, dear friends; with the Lord a day is like a thousand years, and a thousand years are like a day." II Peter 3:8 (NIV)

"What was that?" Bradley cried out. If he hadn't been near Jesus, he would have found himself in total despair. *How could something so evil pervade the sanctity of this paradise?*

Jesus stretched out his hand. In a calm, assured voice, he said, "Be gone."

The heavy presence drifted away but not before it sputtered out an evil, devastating threat, "Listen to my words, O Thou Son of God, there is still plenty of misery left behind with which to attack the mother."

"Oh no! Please don't let him hurt my mother," Bradley cried. "Please, friend, help!" Jesus calmed Bradley just by placing his hand on his shoulder. The realization hit Bradley with full force. "She doesn't know I'm alive, does she? She thinks I'm dead! She only thinks of what's left of me in that cold metal jar. Please don't let him hurt my mother!"

Bradley," Jesus said just as calmly, "your mother has the power of our Holy Spirit living within her, and I have sent someone to remind her to put on the full armor of God.[7] Be assured. If she resists the

---

[7]   "Finally, be strong in the Lord and in his mighty power. Put on the full armor of God so that you can take your stand against the devil's schemes. For our struggle is not against flesh and blood, but against the rulers, against the authorities, against the powers of this dark world and against the spiritual forces of evil in the heavenly realms. Therefore, put on the full armor of God, so that when the day of evil comes, you may stand your ground, and after you have done everything, to stand. Stand firm then, with the belt of truth buckled around your waist, with the breastplate of righteousness in place, and with your feet fitted with the readiness that comes from the gospel of peace. In addition to all this, take up the shield of faith, with which you can extinguish all the flaming arrows of the evil one. Take the helmet of salvation and the sword of the Spirit, which is the word of God." Ephesians 6:10-17 (NIV)

devil, he will flee from her.[8] Your nature, Bradley, the miracle of you and I, the miracle of the Trinity is that you have become one with us."[9] Is this why Bradley felt such peace, such acceptance, because he was an integral part of something much bigger than himself? "It is crucial that those still on earth intercede for each other, but it is not a part of their nature to do so. Therefore, they have to depend on my Word. The power of my Word is so piercing that the evil one and his vile serfs have to flee. Through my written and spoken Word, more than enough power is released to accomplish all things for My glory. It is all in My Word, Bradley. Do you remember what I said when we first met? That your earthly life was destroyed because of your lack of knowledge?" Bradley nodded.

"I love all my creation. How could perfect agape love create and then just walk away? I could not, I would not, and I did not. I gave the world an all-encompassing instruction manual. You call it the Bible. But do you see the problem, Bradley?" Bradley thought but could not. "What good is the power of My Word all closed up between the covers of leather-bound books that sit on a shelf and are never opened? The lack of knowledge gathers strength and a momentum of its own and where it can find a foothold, destroys. My creation tries to do the best that it can all by itself. They don't have to do that, Bradley. You didn't have to do that. It was never my intent to leave you to fend for yourself. I would never do that knowing that the evil one is roaming the earth, seeking whom he may devour."[10] Bradley heard sadness in Jesus' voice and, when he looked up, was touched to

---

8   "Submit yourselves, then, to God. Resist the devil and he will flee from you." James 4:7 (NIV)

9   "… that all of them may be one, Father, just as you are in me and I am in you. May they also be in us so that the world may believe that you have sent me. I have given them the glory that you gave me, that they may be one as we are one." John 17:21 (NIV)

10   "Be self-controlled and alert. Your enemy the devil prowls around like a roaring lion looking for someone to devour." I Peter 5:8 (NIV)

see great remorse on His face. "My saints on earth are on their knees, interceding. Intercession creates miracles. My Word comes to life and will save my hurting, confused, and misled creation. What Lucifer intended for evil, Bradley, I intend for good. Many lives will be saved in memory of you."

Bradley was amazed. He understood more clearly why his new eternal friend had gone to planet earth to live and die and be raised again He knew that from now on, he would be honoring and worshiping Him with every breathe he took. That made him stop and consider. Was he breathing? He must be, he was still alive. But his body had changed. It was more of a presence than flesh and blood.

"In due time, you will get a brand-new body, Bradley. A body that will never decay," Jesus stated matter-of-factly, having once again read Bradley's thoughts.

"May I ask a question, friend?"

Jesus laughed a hearty, warm, and joyful laugh. "You may ask all the questions you'd like, Bradley. There may not be time to answer them all right now, but you will have eternity to discover and learn and find all the answers."

Bradley turned over in his mind how to ask without offending or seeming ungrateful for what he now had. Jesus waited. "I was just wondering. If you knew before I was born that I would go through this tragedy and cause such grief to so many, why did you even let me be born?"

Jesus smiled. "What do you feel right now, Bradley?"

Bradley took in his surroundings, then his state of mind, his emotions, and his intellect. It was all intact. *How did this make him feel?* So many wonderful ways: peaceful, contented, and excited. The list of positive emotions was too long to even consider. But it could be summed up in one word—joy.

"I feel *joy*."

Jesus reached out and hugged him close. "Yes, Bradley, joy. When I was on your earth, I had already been privy to this joy[11] so I knew what waited before me. But you were not privileged to that. You and all the rest of my creation has to depend on hope and build on faith even under what seems to be insurmountable odds. Faith wavers. Hope can be dashed by the evil one. It's hard on earth. Those who stay faithful by believing in me will also experience this joy, forever. Bradley, would you give this up?"

"Oh, never, my friend. Never ever."

"So was it worth it now that you are living in pure joy?" Jesus gave him several flashbacks. Flashbacks that hurt. Flashbacks that, at the time, forced him to feel that life wasn't worth living.

When the flashbacks faded, Bradley said an astounding thing. "Having this complete joy and fullness was worth every pain and sorrow on earth. I would go through it all again a thousand times now that I know this is the reward."

Jesus smiled and hugged Bradley close to him again. "That is very wise of you, Bradley." Jesus arose from the rock they had been sitting on and suggested, "Why don't you take a walk down this path now, Bradley. There are many people waiting to greet you. Remember, you and I have all of eternity to talk."

In the distance, Bradley could see a crowd of people walking up the path toward him. A whole crowd just to see him! He tried to make out the faces, searching for that one special one.

"Is there someone you would truly love to see again, Bradley?" Jesus asked tenderly.

"Yes. Yes, there is," Bradley replied hopefully. Bradley continued to stare down the pathway. The faces were coming into truer

---

[11] "Let us fix our eyes on Jesus, the author and perfecter of our faith. who for the joy set before him endured the cross, scorning its shame, and sat down at the right hand of the throne of God." Hebrews 12:2 (NIV)

focus. And there he was. He wasn't walking with the others. He was running, running to gather up his son in his arms. "Dad!" Bradley shouted. He began racing down the pathway toward him.

As he ran, he heard Jesus' voice in his ear. "After this celebration of you, Bradley, come and see me again. I have a special gift for you." *A gift? For me? A special gift from Jesus just for me?* "Yes, Bradley. Along with eternal life, I have a new name for you as well."[12]

Bradley thought he would explode from all the joy. Instead, he exploded into his earthly father's arms, and then the party began.

---

[12] "He who has an ear, let him hear with the Spirit says to the churches. To him who overcomes, I will give some of the hidden manna. I will also give him a white stone with a new name written on it, known only to him who receives it." Revelation 2:17 (NIV)

Green Fields

She reappeared just as suddenly as she disappeared.

He had just hoisted the last hay bale over the fence into the pasture of restless cows. As was his habit, he looked across the glen toward the stone bridge that crossed McCleary Slough. There she was, like a statue, watching him from their bridge, the bridge where she had thrown flower petals up into the air laughing with delight as she watched them float gently down into the slow-moving water. It was the bridge they had chased each other across, the bridge that led them from the village down into their sacred hollow of dense, gray willows where it would have taken days for anyone to find them had they wanted to be found.

He froze. His insides were churning and his knees wanted to buckle as they stared at each other across the clover-filled meadow. The longer he stared, the more she seemed to be shrinking and receding farther and farther away. Was she just an illusion? He realized he was losing his equilibrium. Just the week before he had finally resigned himself to the fact that she was never coming home. Ever since then, he had been cleansing his mind of memories and his heart of emotions. To see her there now, silhouetted against the twilight of the setting sun, was surreal. He stretched his neck in small indiscernible circles until she came back into focus.

Without taking her eyes from his, she began walking slowly down the curved arc of the bridge, running her hand along the top of the rocked wall. His heart jumped into his throat when he could no longer see her as she stepped from the bridge and moved out of sight behind Alistair's livery stable where the cobblestone street would lead her into the township. He calculated the time it should take for her to walk through the edge of the village and reappear at the top of the knoll leading back to him, a good three minutes at the pace she was walking. Maybe she wasn't coming back to him at all. Maybe she came back just to visit her parents and would be leaving again by morning light. He panicked. He took several strides forward and then caught himself. His pride would let him go no further, so he waited with trepidation, his jaw clenched and his arms hanging slack at his side..

He saw the top of her head first as she came over the rise. Her auburn hair was tied up in a kerchiefed knot with a mass of small curls trying to escape in every possible direction. It was just as he remembered. Then he saw her eyes fixed steadily on his and her wonderful mouth, set in the dewy glow of her Irish complexion. His heart ached. There was no longer light and laughter in her eyes. There was no longer a smile on her lips. She looked the same yet different. He was mesmerized. He could do nothing but stare as she walked slowly toward him. Just out of arm's reach, he realized her face was a fountain of tears. She was shaking and quietly sobbing. It was almost more than he could bare. He still loved her so. She crumbled into a heap at his feet, covering her eyes with her delicate hands as she continued to sob. In a daze of emotions, he reached down, scooped her into his arms, and carried her up the stone steps into the cottage. He placed her gently on the ottoman next to the overstuffed armchair and wrapped a mohair lap blanket snugly around her shoulders. Her face was still in her hands, and her soft sobs were setting all his raw nerves on fire. It was difficult to tell which of them was shaking the most.

Like wildfire, the entire village knew she was back and where she was headed. Speculation and whisperings ran rampant. By the time she reached his small farm, the whole countryside was abuzz.

The embers in the fireplace were barely discernible. He strode over to the hearth and threw on more kindling and several pieces of seasoned pine. When he turned, he found her watching him intently. She opened her mouth to speak, but he raised his right palm to silence her. This was not the time for words.

She could barely see him through her tears. From the moment their eyes met across the meadow, she became numb. How had she done this to him? To them? What could she ever say to be worthy of his forgiveness? She pulled the blanket more tightly around her and sat in silence, breathing in deeply as he passed by to open the curtain between the living room and the loo. His scent was still captivating. The deep, musky draw of his skin quickened her senses. She stared at the strength of his form as he bent down and turned both faucets to fill the claw-footed tub with water, then reach up into the cabinet, and remove a small glass vial that she recognized immediately. She considered the significance as he tapped droplets of lavender into the bathwater. *He kept it all this time.* Her tears began to flow anew.

He went to her side and pulled her gently to her feet, holding her shoulders firmly for an instant as he gazed into her eyes. She trembled as he removed the blanket and carefully pulled the pale-blue Argyle sweater over her head. Turning her around, he snapped open her undergarment, letting it drop to the floor. Then in one swift motion, he removed both her skirt and panties and kicked them into a pile. He bent down and pulled off her shoes. He gathered up all her belongings, opened the front door, and hurled them with great force in the general direction of the burn pile. When he returned, she was still standing where he had left her, skin glowing from the warmth of the fire. He choose not to focus on the beauty of her nakedness. Instead, he walked toward her and lifted her into his arms. She rested her head on his shoulder as he carried her to the tub and set her gently in the water. How many tears could one body hold? Still, they flowed down her chest and into the warm water. He pulled up a three-legged stool and shut off the faucets. He reached for the washcloth with one hand and the bar of soap with the other, then began tenderly washing her. He raised up each arm and stroked the suds over her breasts and back. He washed every part of her completely and with purpose. He was cleansing her. Her tears subsided momentarily as she relaxed into his touch. With each dip of his strong, calloused hands into the water and soft stroke of the cloth over her body, she felt the dirt and the dirtiness begin to slip away.

He refused to let his mind wander. His focus on ridding her of past indiscretions, past sins, and past memories that didn't include him became an immediate obsession. He hadn't meant to slip over into roughness but all too soon, the question of how many times and how many men burst to the forefront. Not until he heard her renewed sobbing did he realize where he had gone in his own grim fantasies and reached out to place her head on his chest. She, in turn, reached up and placed her hand on his cheek. In overpowering remorse, they remained clinging to each other, choking down their own private despair. No words yet spoken as none were needed.

A loud, guttural cry roused him back to reality. It was his cry, a cry of anguish and fear. Fear of what he hadn't been able to suppress in the past and fear of what he might not be able to suppress in the future. He pulled the tub drain and walked over to the wardrobe where he still kept all her clothing. He retrieved her favorite night-gown. She used to curl her legs and feet up into its pink flannel soft-ness as she slept in his arms. He thought he saw a flickering of light in her eyes when she saw it. He tenderly dried her quivering body, slipped the gown over her head, and carried her to their bed. He laid her down gently and crawled in fully clothed beside her, taking her in his arms as he pulled the down comforter around them.

The sun had long since left the western sky. The only light and sound came from the crackling fireplace. They lay in silence for a very long time. She started to speak at one time, but he placed his fingers against her lips and stopped her. One wrong word could snap the thin emotional line they were both straddling. Another time, she raised her face to be kissed. He turned away ever so slightly. She knew then that waiting on him was her only option. As they lay together in that comfortable but precarious state, he felt her body give way to deep sleep. She was safe. She could let it all go in the shelter of his arms. Feeling her warmth and relaxing into her smells, he gently stroked her hair as the reel of remembrance began to play.

He had given her his heart the first time he saw her. She was thirteen; he was fourteen. The new girl in town was traveling with her parents and baby sister all the way from Dublin so her father could take over the position of postmaster after Mr. Conner died. He had been rushing from the first floor to the second at McKenzie High so he wouldn't be late once again for class. He smiled now as he remembered barreling around the corner and smacking into her so hard they both landed on the floor. Those deep-green eyes meeting his light-brown ones was all it took. "Goodness!" had been her only response. At that point, he didn't care if he ever attended class again. All he wanted was to grab her hand, lead her back down the stairs and outside into the warm spring air, take her for a walk on the bridge, and discover everything about her, anything that would keep her from walking away from him to get to her own class. But that was exactly what she did. The only thing she left him was a back-glance smile. He was so smitten, he didn't even hear the last bell ring. He just stood there staring after her. He suddenly felt like a man in his fourteen-year-old body. He couldn't quite comprehend all the emotions he was having, but he did know with all certainty she was his destiny.

The reel was playing in slow motion. Her cheering while he made touchdown after touchdown, family picnics by the lake, church socials, discovering their secret place in the pines, their first kiss. They came to know each other inside out. She loved to debate, especially with him. The topics included everything from why chickens didn't care that the rooster had a harem to who would win the next mayoralty election and why that was or was not a good thing. Why did she win every debate? She wasn't any smarter than him. She just had a way about her. He reveled giving in because he just wanted her to be happy. They laughed, they had spats, and they wouldn't speak to each other for days at a time because she was so frustratingly stubborn and would not budge an inch until he saw things her way. Everyone in town knew they were soul mates, would eventually marry, have a dozen kids, and go on forever. Everyone but the new kid who showed up his senior year. He learned the hard way when he ended up with a black eye. They did marry. The church was filled. The bells were ringing. The village was smiling. Their happily-ever-after began with great joy.

Then one day, not long after, there was a note on the kitchen table. "Please forgive me. I love you." Even as he stood there in disbelief, he knew.

He felt her stir and pressed her more tightly to him. Where had they gone wrong? More importantly, why? It began with small, subtle incidents. She began buying gossip magazines and became enamored with the celebrity lifestyle. She talked more frequently about her desire to travel across the ocean and visit Hollywood, maybe even become a movie star. Soon, the reality of them, their lives, their dreams was replaced with the greener grass of her fantasies. Maybe he shouldn't have laughed it off. Maybe he should have saved up their money so he could have taken her on that trip instead of buying the secondhand combine that was still costing him more on repairs than the original price. All the maybes in the world lay limp and futile. He needed to focus on the now, the future. He felt his face flush as he once again dove headfirst into his own fantasies. He shook her gently but firmly enough to rouse her.

"How many?"

She heard the words but hid her face in his chest, not wanting to answer. He waited. "Five"

It was only after she was gone that he learned she left with that smooth-talking, slicked-back Fuller Brush salesman. He wanted to kick himself for not wondering why her trips to the mercantile were taking longer and longer each week. It answered the question of where she could come up with that kind of travel money. With the turn of a screw, his life turned upside down. He could stand up to being the never-ending topic of conversation in the village, but he couldn't stomach the pity. There was not a word from her or about her in two long years—years of sorrow and regret and days upon days of agonizing and allowing tormented fantasies to take over his life. Two long years. Years in which he did nothing but go through the motions. Go find her, people said. Divorce her, people said. Get on with your life, people said. Without looking even more of a fool, how could he make them understand that she was his life?

The number *five* began swirling around in his head. It might as well have been five thousand. He threw off the covers, his feet landing on the floor with a loud thud. She barely stirred as she rolled over and buried her head into the goose-down pillow. He stared at her. Could love turn so quickly to hate? No. There was no hate, but he felt bile rising up in his throat and an overwhelming sense of revulsion. He wanted names, he wanted locations, and he wanted a gun.

She awoke the next morning with the sun shining on her face as it peeked through the slit in the curtain. Fully awake, she looked to his side of the bed. He was not there. She slipped out of bed and lifted his robe from the bench, pulling it tightly around her. The sound of an ax splintering wood drifted in through the open kitchen door. She walked over and gazed at him through the screen. There was a sheen of sweat on his shirtless back and forearms, and his muscles bulged with each new swing of the ax. The burn pile was smoldering. She thought she saw the sole of one of her shoes in among the ashes.

He finished chopping the last piece of pinewood and carried it over to where four other logs were stacked next to the fire. Kneeling down, he blew on the embers until the swirling air ignited once again into flames. He threw on several pieces of kindling and stood rigidly staring into the fire. When the burn became hot and steady, he reached down to pick up one of the logs, raised it above his head and heaved it with all the force he had into the middle of the flames. Sparks danced heavenward and ashes rained down all over his body, but he didn't seem to notice.

A sob caught in her throat. The irony of his actions was not lost on her. Five logs, five indiscretions. She watched in silence as he began burning up her past. She didn't want to think about all the things she told him the night before. He insisted on knowing not just every name, but every detail within every detail. He could tell when she was hedging or softening the facts and he made her start all over again each time until he was sure the truth was out. It had been exhausting.

Her first wide-eyed opportunity came via the Fuller Brush man who ditched her unceremoniously once they reached California. Then there was the talent scout who could not stop praising her natural beauty and promised her big parts in big pictures if she would only sleep with him. He would take care of her, he said. That care stopped the moment she gave in. Then there was the rape, the details of which were so devastating that she hyperventilated in its telling. Next came an actual boyfriend. He was good to her. They made plans. She wavered on writing a Dear John letter but only briefly. He didn't know she was married. What shocked her back to her senses? The evening he proposed and professed his undying love and desire to be married, make a home together, and start a family. What in the world was she doing? What in the world was she thinking? There was only one man in the world with whom she wanted to have children, and he was back in Ireland along with her heart. She didn't consider the final indiscretion an indiscretion at all. It was a necessity, pure and simple. She had to get back to Ireland. She had no money; he did. She moved in with him for six months; he became abusive after two. There didn't seem to be an escape route away from him. He controlled her every move, her comings and goings. The last night before escaping him, she gave an award-winning performance—the kind she had once dreamed of accomplishing in Hollywood—with insincere laughter, coddling, and submission. He was so narcissistic, he didn't know the difference. She was very cautious when she continuously poured her drinks into his when he wasn't looking. When the aperitifs and bottles of wine were gone, he passed out into a sated stupor. There was no bag to pack. She wanted nothing of him, only his money, so she had no qualms with taking the eight one-hundred dollar bills from his wallet. She avoided the street lights and sprinted the half mile to a pay phone where she called a taxi. Her ticket was in hand, and the plane boarded before the sun came up.

Now here she stood, staring through the screen, still aching deep inside, and fighting down unpredictable sobs. There was no indication one way or the other as to how this would end. He got up from the rock and was on the porch in two quick steps. He opened the screen door and brushed past her without a word. She heard him rummaging around in the loo, the chest of drawers in the bedroom, then back to the kitchen where he lifted several items from under the kitchen sink. He was sullen and focused, as if in a trance. She stepped out of his path as he banged through the door and stormed back down to the burn pile. She wasn't sure he even knew she was there. She bit her lip as she watched him hurl all the items into the fire, poking them into the flames until the heat consumed them. Each item was stamped with the same damning logo—Fuller Brush. When the log was no longer distinguishable from the dirt beneath it, he rose slowly and picked up the second log. He didn't move for several minutes, he just stared. Suddenly, as if he could no longer carry the weight, he dropped it on the ground. Then he kicked it with such force that it catapulted into the air, landed on the crest of a slope, and began rolling down an incline. In one swift motion, he was beside it, kicking it again and again as it continued to roll. She sank to the floor as she watched this mad man kicking and screaming obscenities as his heavy work boots pummeled the log from one end of the field to the other.

He was seething with hate. Hate that someone had tricked her, used her, and quashed her dreams. But more than anything, he was kicking himself for not having been able to realize them for her. He half stumbled back up the incline, panting for breath as he carried the log back to the fire. Once again, he hurled it with all his might into the midst of the flames and did not move until it was no more. The third log had slipped down between the last two and was sticking straight up, mocking him. His fists clenched and unclenched but he made no move toward it. He just stood and sneered at it. Finally, he strode toward the pile, pushed the two horizontal logs to the side, and knocked the offending log into the fire with his boot. He didn't want to touch it.

His next action frightened her to the point that she unconsciously backed away from the door. The ax was resting against the tree where he had left it. He walked over to it and then back to the fire. Strange animal sounds began working their way up from his throat. He raised the ax and swung down hard, chopping the log in two and splintering it into smaller and smaller pieces. He cut off its legs, its arms, its manhood. Over and over, the ax came down. The fire raged out of control, singeing his pants and sending sparks up to his face. He was possessed. He didn't even notice the burning and charring of his exposed skin. A flame leaped so high that it caught a low-hanging tree branch on fire; still, he chopped and annihilated. When he was totally spent, he hurled the ax across the drive and plopped down on a rock. He was still oblivious to the pain from the minor burns on his arms and chest but he did notice the tree branch on fire. With a heavy grunt, he walked over to the garden hose and doused out the unintended fire.

He glanced at the fourth log and quickly looked away. Of course he knew she was gone, but he had never really accepted that she would leave him forever—and she almost had. For whom? How was he better? The others had hurt his pride, his ego. This one hurt his heart. Dear John. What would he have done if that Dear John letter had arrived? He hung his head.

She wondered how long this would go on. It was already late afternoon. How much more could either of them bear? Yet two logs remained, and she knew he would not stop until they were destroyed. She wanted to rush to his side, take his face in her hands, and somehow convince him it had been nothing. It had been a thoughtless, cruel game, and she cared not for that man. But she knew he had to come to terms with each indiscretion in his own right. She was suddenly so very weary. She wanted it all to be over. Not just this day of purging, but the last two years gone, vanishing into thin air as if they had never happened. She was consumed with guilt.

Slowly, he got up from the rock, walked over to the log, and placed it in the fire. There were no flames left intact. The log just lay there. *Is that how it would always be? A place in her heart for another man that wouldn't burn out?* He felt like a small child again, wanting to hide in the folds of his mother's apron. Instead, he built the fire back up and watched as the log took its own prolonged time to burn into cinders.

From where he was sitting, the final log looked out of proportion, bigger than the rest and more gnarled with some of its bark beginning to peel away. He choked down the bile he felt rising again. It made sense now—those bruises on her arms and back when he had given her a bath. Nothing he could do would be severe enough to expel the imagery of what she had gone through. He sank to the ground as he envisioned her soft, frail body being abused. His love, his wife. It no longer mattered what she had done and where she had been. His only thought was that he wasn't there to protect her. His imaginings became more vivid until he thought he would go insane. He rushed to the log and hurled it into the fire. Then he disappeared into the shed and when he returned, he had a gas can in his hands.

She was horrified. Before she had a chance to move or cry out to stop him, she heard him scream, "Burn in Hell" as he doused the fire with half the contents from the can. The entire burn blew into the sky, engulfing his surroundings in flames. Was this what he had been leading up to, making her watch him die? Paying her back with such vengeance? She was already on the porch, beginning to descend the stairs when he miraculously stepped out of the flames unscathed. In disbelief, she grabbed on the railing for support and tried to keep from fainting. He tossed the can aside and sank to the ground, head in hands, sobs racking his body. She thought her heart would burst from her chest, yet she stood frozen, her knuckles white from gripping the rail. Only after he let out a loud, husky groan was she able to take a deep breath.

He got up from the ground and turning looked straight at her. It was the first time he had acknowledged her all day. He looked different now. The mad man was gone. The manic expression was replaced with a tranquil countenance. His eyes were clear and unclouded, and they were beckoning her. He knew from the moment he saw her on the bridge that she would be his again. He knew without a doubt that this too was her desire. He stood tall and commanding, waiting for her to come to him, and she did. As they melted into each other's embrace, he whispered softly but firmly into her ear, "It is done. We shall speak of it no more."

She had returned. He had waited.

> "Go, show your love to your wife again, though she
> is loved by another and is an adulteress. Love her
> as the Lord loves the Israelites, though they turn to
> other gods and love the sacred raisin cakes."
> —Hosea 3:1 (NIV)

Chaff

is eyes were closed, his head tilted upward as he took deep, satiating breaths of the cool air stirring gently around him. Seconds before, he had been panicked in suffocation, unable to catch even the slightest of breaths, but now his lungs were filling with sweet fragrance like that near a mountain stream. He breathed in deeply and smiled. He opened his eyes and let out a cry of surprise when he realized he was suspended in midair. His legs went into a furious dog paddle as he reached out both arms, grasping desperately at nothing. At the same moment, he felt a strong grip under his left elbow that steadied his flailing limbs, shifting his mind from agitation to calmness.

Immediately, he knew without being told. He had died but somehow was still alive. He shouldn't have been shocked but he was. He strongly believed that someday he would enter the reality of this supernatural dimension, but not at the age of forty-five and definitely not due to a heart attack. His amazement of actually being here was more than disconcerting. His last earthly memory was that of white sheets, tubes, and bleeping machinery. As his spirit lifted out of his physical body, he remembered looking down at his family standing by his bedside, trying to be brave.

With forehead resting on the pillow, his wife had been holding his hand and sobbing, "Please don't go, John, please don't go!"

Now they were all in a different reality from his, but he had no fear. He knew he would see them again, and it gave him great peace. He looked up into the face of the angel who was holding his arm. It was a strong, resolute face, a face filled with contentment.

The angel looked back at him and smiled. "I am your guide," he stated matter-of-factly.

"Where are we going?"

The angel looked down at him with warm, sky-blue eyes but did not respond. He just smiled once again. John chuckled to himself. He knew exactly where they were headed—to the pearly gates of heaven. He could hardly wait. How considerate of God to provide a guide so he wouldn't lose his way. Little did he know that the angel's presence was for an even greater purpose. Afar off, an intense golden glow filled the sky. The heavens seemed to be churning in a way he imagined a volcano would look close up with billows of reds, oranges, and yellows toppling over each other in swirling twists and turns.

"What is that ahead?" he asked his chaperone.

"That is the cleansing fire, the eternal fire that burns up all chaff. All humans who believe and accept our Lord, the Christ, must go through it to purge themselves. It is the almighty fire of God."

John wasn't sure he liked the sound of that. Would it hurt? Would his guardian stay with him? From the still firm grip on his elbow, he assumed so. As the remembrance of his physical world began to slip away, he became more aware of his new reality and surroundings. He realized he was not the only human being transported toward the fire in the sky. He glanced to his right and met the eyes of another man who returned his gaze in wonder. There were women and children and more men of all ages surrounding him but ambivalent towards him as they focused on their own private journey. Feeling completely at ease with his guide, he wondered if he was allowed to ask questions.

As if reading his mind, the angel smiled down at him once again and stated, "Ask whatever you'd like. It is my appointment to administer peace and answer questions."

"Well," John ventured somewhat timidly, sensing that he should have been a better student of the Bible while on planet Earth and already know the answers. "Once I believed and accepted Christ as my Savior, I thought I was already purged from my sin because of the blood he shed on the cross."

"That is absolute truth," replied the angel. "This purging through fire is yet another of God's gifts along with our Christ's gift of salvation."

This gave John pause for thought. He knew the angel would explain more fully but until then, that statement triggered more questions than it answered. He watched in awe as they glided slowly but purposefully toward the fire. They were so close now he wondered why he felt no heat from the churning billows. He thought back to the bonfires he, his wife, and his two sons built on the beach during the long, cool evenings of autumn. While sitting on logs around the fire enjoying hot dogs and sodas, they could feel the heat from only two or three feet away and this fire was enormously bigger than a bonfire.

John stared as the people in front of him drifted into the fire and disappeared as if into a thick fog bank. Instinctively, he stiffened and grasped the angel's forearm with his right hand. "Will this hurt?" he asked, more from amazement than fear.

"Only during the fleeting moment of regret," the angel replied. Suddenly, they were in the midst of the intense, glowing light, giving John no time to wonder about the angel's comment. He would discover that meaning soon enough. He felt the angel release his elbow.

"This you must do alone," he said as he gently pushed him deeper into the fire.

Having been a civil engineer on earth and very analytical, John was quick to deduce that he still felt no heat and, amazingly, no fear. He took comfort in the angel's words, "It is a gift from God." He knew that God gives good gifts to His children so what was there to fear? Part of Psalm 63 came to mind. "Your right hand upholds me."[1] He was thankful for that memory as he waited expectantly.

Then the purging began. Weighty thoughts and images bombarded him. He remembered the old adage, "At death, your whole life flashes before your eyes." That seemed to be happening now. From birth through death, thoughts and images were projected with lightning speed and, just as quickly, shot above his head in a dizzying, spinning pattern. John realized in an instant that none of these thoughts, let alone the images, were pleasing to God. They ran the gamut of shameful to slothful, from laziness to indifference. There was cursing and there was lust. Along with anger, there was bitterness and resentment. They were, in fact, all useless and all garbage. He was quite remorseful to relive them. As the onslaught of purging continued, he saw a shape moving toward him. It came to a hovering rest a few feet in front of him, and John realized it was the scales of justice. Both the right and left pans were empty and evenly balanced. The atmosphere around him began to vibrate and quiver as a piercing hum filled the air. He watched as the swirling mass of thoughts and images traveled toward the scales and landed rather violently on the left pan, causing it to sink well below the central pillar while raising the right pan higher than the top of the beam. Mesmerized, he continue to watch as rainbow-colored flecks began to descend into the right pan. He immediately recognized his moments of joy, love, compassion, and the fruits of the Spirit he tried to put into practice

---

[1] "My soul clings to you; your right hand upholds me" Psalm 63:8 (NIV)

while on earth as they fell into the pan. His heart sank. The right pan barely moved.

Regret overwhelmed him. This was the pain forewarned by his angel. It was so powerful that had he not been suspended in mid-air, it would have dropped him to his knees. The point was brought home like a sledgehammer. He looked at the left pan and hung his head. Why had he wasted so much time focused on things that did not matter eternally, things that he could not take with him? Why had he filled his life with egotism and selfish pride? Why had he wasted so much precious time pursuing earthly gain and personal pleasures? It was obvious none of that waste was going to follow him into heaven. He wanted to sob. He wanted to go back and have a chance to even the scales. A verse in the book of Matthew crossed his mind, "Do not store up for yourselves treasures on earth, where moth and rust destroy and where thieves break in and steal. But store up for yourselves treasures in heaven."[22] Not only had he let himself down, he had let Jesus down. He shivered to think that Jesus had been a witness to his earthly carnality. At that moment, he saw another shape moving toward him through the haze of the fire. It was a miniature rendering of a wooden cross—the cross upon which Jesus hung and the cross that had the power to conquer Satan and sin. It was the cross of Golgotha. Its descent was steady, yet gentle as it touched down into the right pan like snow falling onto a goose down pillow. However, upon impact, the right pan dropped instantly and resolutely, causing the left pan to spring up violently and spew its contents high into the air. John watched as each worthless thought and image floated past him and began to sink deep into the abyss of

---

[2]   "Lay not up for yourselves treasures upon earth, where moth and rust doth corrupt, and thieves break through and steal; but, lay up for yourselves treasures in heaven, where neither moth nor rust doth corrupt and where thieves do not break through nor steal." Matthew 6:19-20 (NIV)

God's almighty fire below him. One by one, they vaporized into a puff of smoke.

He was engulfed by the sound of a thunderous voice, "As far as the east is from the west, I will remove your sins from you."[33] With that, he suddenly found himself on the other side of the fire, surrounded by a pure, white light. He felt strong and whole, like a stalk of wheat swaying gently in the breeze yet planted firmly in the ground. Once again, he heard the thunderous voice of God, "With my winnowing fork, I have cleared my threshing floor. I have gathered my wheat into the barn and burned up the chaff with unquenchable fire."[44]

He turned and looked, but the fire was not there. When he looked ahead, looming large in the distance were the gates of heaven. He could not distinguish faces yet but it was obvious that people were laughing and waving to him, encouraging him to hurry. As John made his way to join the masses, he was filled with awe, finally understanding that the gift of life God bestowed on him was for all eternity, not just the forty-five years he spent on earth. He raised his arms to the sky. "Thank you, Father-God!" he cried out.

It had become crystal clear that from everlasting to everlasting, it really was all about Jesus. Without the power of His crucifixion, His dominion over sin and Satan, and His resurrection, none of this would be possible. He was amazed at the simplicity of the two-step plan of salvation: God's amazing grace and Jesus' miraculous sacrifice.

Then he heard the whisper of God in his ear. "You missed a step, John. The most vital step. You are here with me forever because of step number three."

---

[3]   "As far as the east is from the west, so far has he removed our transgressions from us." Psalm 103:12 (NIV)

[4]   "His winnowing fork is in his hand to clear his threshing floor and to gather the wheat into his barn, but he will burn up the chaff with unquenchable fire." Luke 3:17 (NIV)

John did not have to think hard to understand God's meaning. Belief. Another Bible verse popped into his mind, "Believe on the Lord Jesus Christ, and you shall be saved."[55] Everything made sense now that he realized what an important part he played in God's plan because of his belief and his acceptance of Christ as Savior. God didn't even make it difficult. Believe, simply believe. To bring the plan full circle, there was that third step, that one vital detail—mankind's faith. John's faith. Without the childlike faith of believing in what God did, the circle had a gaping break in it. The plan was incomplete. He knew for certain that the cost was very high for the triune God, but everything had been set in place before the creation of man. All the garbage wasn't a surprise to Almighty God. *He was and is and always shall be omnipotent, omniscient, and omnipresent,* John thought. He took care of the sinful state of man before it could even present itself.

God began talking to him intimately, one-on-one. "John, I knew you could never live a flawless life, let alone a perfect one. But I loved you even before you were in your mother's womb.[66] The solution to that quandary was My Son being willing to die just for you. His perfection covered all your imperfections. Don't yearn to go back and try harder to make your life more pure. Try as you might, you could never accomplish that. I do not even see those earthly sins. All I see is you covered in righteousness because of My Son's shed blood over you."[77]

---

5   "I tell you the truth, whoever hears my word and believes him who sent me has eternal life and will not be condemned; he has crossed over from death to life." John 5:24 (NIV)

6   "For you created my inmost being; you knit me together in my mother's womb." Psalm 139:13 (NIV)

7   "Blessed is he whose transgressions are forgiven, whose sins are covered. Blessed is the man whose sin the Lord does not count against him and in whose spirit is no deceit." Psalm 32:1-2 (NIV)

John smiled. Suddenly, the excitement was overwhelming. He could hardly wait to meet Jesus and see God, not just hear his voice. He wondered what the Holy Spirit looked like. He definitely wanted to have a long sit-down talk with Noah, maybe around a heavenly camp fire, and Abraham and Moses and Paul, for sure. He could spend years listening to Paul. Oh my goodness, Adam and Eve were high on his list! His mind was racing as the list grew longer and longer.

"You will have all eternity to meet your ancestors, to learn and grow, and to understand. You will never tire of seeking knowledge. All things will be made clear, and your joy will be complete and never-ending. Because you believed, John, all because you believed. Thank you, John. I am thrilled to be your God. Welcome to paradise."

*   *   *